IT WAS YOU

KIM HARTFIELD

IT WAS YOU

.

One – Ella

Some families are normal. One husband, one wife, two-point-five kids, and a white picket fence. Mom cooks dinner every night, they all eat together while politely discussing their days, and then the kids wash up while Dad relaxes on the couch with a beer.

Then there are families like mine.

"Heads up!" Sam launched a snowball at my head.

I dipped down and grabbed a handful of the white stuff, ignoring the way it soaked through my thin gloves as I formed it into a ball. "Back at you, prick!"

Coco raced in front of him, jumping to slap the snowball down before it could find its target. "Not on my watch."

"Oh, you're taking Sam's side, are you?" I advanced on my kid sister, picking up another handful of snow. "You two can team up if you want. I'm still going to take you down!"

"Not a chance," Sam said, flicking loose snow in my direction. "I could take on both of you with my hands tied behind my back."

"Yeah right, dipshit." I kicked up a cloud of snow. "I'm the undisputed champion of snowball fights, in case you've forgotten since last year."

He'd surprised me with a snowball on my way home from work every day, and it'd spiraled into a full-on war. My crowning achievement had been the time I waited for him to get home, letting him think he was safe, and then dumped a bucket full of snow over his head as soon as he came inside the house.

"Kids!" Mom called from the porch.

I turned toward her, my laughter fading. It was annoying that she still referred to us as "kids." Sam and I were grown adults with jobs – I was twenty-four and he was twenty-one – even if we still lived at home. Coco was an actual kid, only nine years old.

"You need to watch your language," Mom said, coming down the porch steps. "And for the record, *I'm* going to be the snowball champion in 2019."

She raced toward us, perfectly molded snowballs already in her hands. She whipped one at Sam, hitting him smack in the face. Another flew at Coco, who was too stunned to duck.

Well, she wasn't going to get me. I ducked – but she must've anticipated the movement, because next thing I knew I was spitting out snow.

"Dammit!" I yelled. "That doesn't count."

"Again, honey, language," Mom said sweetly as

another snowball hit me square in the chest.

Oh, well. I'd make lemons out of lemonade. "Since I'm wet anyway, I'm going to make a snow angel," I said, flopping down to the ground. "And since you're still dry, Madam Snowball Champion, you won't mind making dinner."

It was my night to make it. Sam and I usually traded off; cooking was one of the chores we did in order to live here rent-free. The deal worked out well for all of us. Mom always had someone around to look after Coco, which was a big help since none of our dads were around anymore. And Sam and I could save money instead of spending it on rent.

"Fine, I'll cook," Mom said. "I need one assistant, though. Somebody to chop and stir."

If she was trying to imply that should be me, it wasn't working. "I volunteer Coco," I said, moving my arms and legs along the ground. "She needs to practice her skills more than Sam or me."

"That's not fair," Coco said.

"Life's not fair," Sam said, flopping down at my side. "I'm all wet now, too. I can't go in."

Coco's brow furrowed. "What if I…"

"Nope! You can make snow angels *after* dinner." Grabbing her arm, Mom tugged her inside.

I moved my head lazily from side to side,

making a big head for my angel. The snow was fluffy and fresh, and so white that it glittered in the bright sun. Soon I'd be sick of this weather, but this was the first snowfall of the season, and it felt magical.

"We're not going to go crazy this year," I said, squinting at Sam as he worked on his angel. "I'm not having a full-on war. I have too much going on in my life. I don't want to be worrying that I'm going to get soaked on my way to work in the morning."

"You're no fun," he said playfully. "Mom wants to take your title. Coco's old enough to have a fighting chance, too."

"I'll give up the title if it means I won't have to be hit with snowballs at random times." I stood up and took a look at my handiwork. The snow angel was a little lopsided, but not bad for a first try.

"We'll see." Sam got up, too. His angel looked even worse than mine. "I don't want to show up to work all wet, either. I just got a cute girl's number, and I'm trying to make a good impression before I start my new job."

I cut my eyes toward him. "Really? A coworker?"

He scuffed a foot over his angel's foot. "Yeah, we've kind of been dancing around each other for a while. I figured things can't get too messy since I'll be leaving the job in two weeks anyway. I finally asked for her number, and she actually gave it to me."

"I didn't know you had a crush!"

Most brothers might not have told their sisters about stuff like this, but like I said, we weren't the average family. Sam's love interests were frequently the subject of dinner-table conversation during our high school years, and we teased him endlessly about them. Even Coco got in on the jokes.

They'd teased me about boys for most of my life, then been thrown off a few years ago when I told them they should've been worrying about girls all along. These days, the three of them made fun of me just as much as Sam. The difference was that I kept my crushes to myself, so they had a lot less ammunition.

"I don't tell you everything," Sam said, narrowing his eyes at me.

The thing was that he normally did. That was who he was – blunt and upfront, simple even. He couldn't keep a secret if his life depended on it. Or was he finally changing?

His job as a barista had never required much from him, aside from the people skills that he innately had. Now that he'd graduated college and was moving on to a "real" job, he'd have to master office politics. Maybe he'd become a whole new person.

"How long has this crush been going on for?" I asked.

"Two weeks. Maybe three."

My shoulders relaxed. Maybe he wasn't becoming a master of deception, after all.

I kicked snow over my angel until it was nothing but a mess on the ground. Heading to a fresh spot, I lay down and started over. "So, who is this girl? What's so great about her?"

"Her name's Judi," Sam said, shoving his hands in his pockets. "She's so cool and funny. She's really smart and nice, and she's into basketball and soccer." He paused. "Oh, and she's really pretty, too."

Hmm... he'd started by listing her personality characteristics rather than what she looked like. "Pretty" was only an afterthought at the end. He really was into this girl.

His love life had been slow since his last break-up several months ago. He'd dated that girl for almost a year, and they'd seemed pretty serious about each other. Our whole family had loved her, and the split had taken us by surprise.

Still, Sam's love life was better than mine. I'd never had an official relationship – only a few dates here and there. It was hard to meet LGBT people when you lived in a small town like Fronton. Half the lesbians I knew were permanently single and biding their time until they could move to a bigger city. The rest were in long-distance relationships with people from Denver, the closest major city. Some of them were dating people they hadn't even met in person.

Fronton was going to have its first Pride festival this summer, which was something. I'd actually signed up to volunteer to organize it. With a little luck, I might meet someone – either another volunteer, or a festival-goer.

At this point in my life, I could use some luck.

"She sounds pretty great," I said. "Have you texted her yet?" I stood up and surveyed my snow angel. It'd turned out slightly better than the last one, although it still might not have looked much like an angel. Icy water was seeping into my clothes, and I shivered and hugged myself.

"No, I haven't." Sam moved to a new spot and lay down again. "I was actually hoping you could do it for me."

"Say what?" I kicked him more gently than I wanted to. "What are you talking about?"

He sat up with a sigh. "This girl is amazing, Ella. Seriously, she's everything I've ever wanted. She could be the real deal."

I hadn't heard him talk about a girl this way since his break-up. Still… "How does that relate to me texting her?"

"You're better with words than me, library lady." He brushed snow off his knees. "She's into ideas and stuff. I want her to think I'm smart, too."

"What is this, a sitcom?" I shook my head. "This kind of thing never works. No matter what I say over text, she's going to interact with you in person eventually. She'll see the real you then."

"Who cares?" Sam asked. "You can make a good first impression, and I'll take it from there. It won't even be a big deal."

I narrowed my eyes at him. He seriously wanted me to do this – and I was starting to actually consider it. It sounded fun, with a little dash of evil. But really, what harm would come of it? Even if I gave him a helping hand, he'd still have to hit it off with Judi in person, or their potential relationship wouldn't go anywhere.

"What's in it for me?" I asked.

He stood up. "I'll do your chores for a week."

I raised an eyebrow. "Which chores?"

"All of them. Cooking, dishes, sweeping, laundry, snow shoveling…"

Now this was getting seriously tempting. "And you won't launch any surprise snowball attacks?" I asked. "Morning, afternoon, or night?"

"I'll even throw some at Mom and Coco if you want me to." He made puppy-dog eyes at me. "*Please,* Ella. I really like this girl."

"All right." I held a hand up before he could get too excited. "Ground rules. I text her long enough to set up your first date. Once it's scheduled, you're on your own. Even if that only takes a day, you still have to do my chores for a week."

I expected it'd be easy to set up a date. If this girl liked him enough to give him her number, surely she'd be willing to go out with him once.

"Okay," Sam said.

"And I was planning to deep-clean the upstairs bathroom this week," I said. "So that's going to be included."

He didn't even blink. "Sure."

He was willing to scrub the toilet for a slightly-increased shot at getting a date with this girl? He was even further gone than I'd thought.

I smiled. I hoped Judi could actually be the love of his life. He deserved some happiness.

And if that meant I might be able to get him to do more housework for me, even better.

Two – Judi

Yawning, I took the used grinds out of the coffee maker and dropped them into the trash. It was finally closing time, and I was ready to lie down in front of the TV and unwind. I'd been on my feet for eight hours straight, with only a ten-minute break for lunch.

I moved out of the way so Wren could close up the cash register. I still had to take the baked goods out of the display case, but I took a moment to pull my phone out of my apron pocket. I hadn't had a chance to check for new messages for an hour or two.

"Waiting to hear from Sam?" Wren asked with a grin.

Although there was a new text, Wren had me feeling self-conscious, and I shoved the phone back into my pocket without looking at it. "Go away."

"Come on, it's adorable. A coffee-shop romance…"

I rolled my eyes. I could've killed Sam for asking me for my number in front of another coworker. Sure, we'd been lightly flirting for a couple of weeks, and I'd guessed the ask might be coming, but couldn't he have done it in private?

He hadn't even been subtle about it. He'd been

telling both of us about how he'd gotten a "real" job and he'd be leaving Caffeine Hut. Then, with a huge grin, he'd turned to me and said, "I guess this is the moment to try my luck. Judi, could I get your number?"

My cheeks went hot all over again as I thought about it.

I stepped behind Wren and grabbed a tray of donuts. "It's not a romance yet. I don't even know if I'm interested."

He wasn't my usual type at all. He seemed like the typical straight guy, a bit of a meathead even, and I had no idea how he'd react when he found out I was bisexual. Being queer was a huge part of my identity, and I'd been volunteering with LGBT organizations for years. Still, he was kind of cute, and we'd gotten along fine so far. I was open to going on a date and seeing if anything came of it.

"Sure, sure." Wren sounded dubious. "And save the sprinkle ones for me."

Getting to take the baked goods home was one of the few perks of working at Caffeine Hut. Six months in, and I'd gained a pants size.

Hopefully one of these days I'd get a grown-up job like Sam had. Too bad I hadn't been thinking about my career prospects when I decided to get my bachelor's degree in gender studies.

I bagged the sprinkle donuts for Wren and a couple of chocolate ones for me. The rest, I covered in plastic wrap and placed in the fridge. A worker from a local charity would come by to pick them up tomorrow.

"I'm all done, if you don't mind locking up," I said, untying my apron and slipping on my winter coat. "See you tomorrow!"

"See you." She looked up at me and winked. "Say hi to Sam for me."

Cursing at her silently, I walked to my car. I checked my phone before even getting inside. Sam's message simply said *Hey you,* with a smiley face.

Hey yourself, I wrote back. *How was your day off? What kind of hijinks did you get up to?*

I got behind the wheel, expecting to see another message from him when I got home. My phone dinged again before I could even put the key in the ignition.

Family snowball fight, he'd written. *There was no clear winner, unfortunately, but this was just the beginning of this year's snow war. Give it some time, and the others will bow down to my wrath!*

I blinked at the screen. He sounded wittier than he did in real life. Maybe he wasn't a total meathead after all.

You can do it! I typed. *You'll be the Snow King before you know it. I had a more boring day – just finished work, and I'm on my way home to crash with some Netflix.*

I reread it to make sure it was clever enough. It

didn't seem as good as his message had been, and I found myself wanting to match wits with him.

Then again, why should I have to impress him? I wasn't even sure if I liked this guy. I hit "send" and drove home, trying not to wonder the whole time about what his response would be.

I gave in to temptation and checked my phone before I got out of my car. Seeing he'd already responded made me feel a little warm inside. Clearly I was more into this guy than I'd thought.

What's good on the 'flix? he'd written.

The 'flix? Who calls it that? I typed. *And I'm not sure. I actually just finished watching Day Parade. Sooo romantic, they were perfect together! Now I'm ready for a new show… any recommendations?*

I headed into the house and said hi to my roommate, Chelle, who was in the living room with her girlfriend Sabrina. Chelle held their bowl of popcorn toward me, and I waved it away. "I just want to crash."

"No worries," Chelle said. "You don't look tired, though. You look excited, if anything."

"Do I?" I blushed.

"Yeah," Sabrina said, sitting up straight to examine me. "It's like you're glowing."

"You two are imagining things."

I beat a hasty retreat to my room. I had a flat

screen connected to my laptop, and I tended to stay in here rather than socializing with them. Although they were both nice and friendly, I tended to like to spend my free time alone – especially because seeing their happiness was a constant reminder of my own singlehood.

I turned the computer on and checked my phone again. Sam was replying so quickly – it seemed like he was really into me. I'd already known he was, but wow. I hadn't been interested in someone who was also interested in me in… well, a long time.

I hadn't prioritized dating for a while now. My last relationship had lasted six months, and it wasn't too serious. The girl was pretty into me, but somehow the feeling wasn't quite right. We weren't *perfect* together, and I didn't want to settle for less than that.

In the end, the girl had moved to the other side of the country to get her master's degree. We'd thought about staying together, and maybe we would've made it work if I was really crazy about her. In the end, we decided the distance would just be too much. We'd cut off contact, and I rarely thought about her at all.

I just watched something amazing, Sam said. *It's not a show, though, it's a documentary. Interested?*

I lay on my front and texted back, *How can I say I'm interested if you didn't tell me anything about it? Tease.*

I scrolled through a few of the offerings on

Netflix. Nothing immediately caught my attention, and I grabbed my phone the second it dinged with a new message.

I don't know if I should tell you, Sam said. *I might scare you off.*

What? Tell me!

Well... it's about a serial killer.

I laughed out loud. I couldn't see Sam sitting down and watching a doc about a serial killer at all! Clearly we had a lot of getting to know each other to do.

I'm shocked! You must be a serial killer yourself. I'm not going to talk to you anymore, I wrote back, and immediately followed up with a second text. *JK. It sounds like it's right up my alley. What's it called?*

Tries, Lies, and Alibis.

I typed in the title and read the summary. This definitely looked appealing – more than watching reruns of *Friends* for the hundredth time. *I'll check it out,* I texted. *Thanks for the rec!*

No problem. I'll let you enjoy it. Drop me a text tomorrow and let me know what you thought.

He was cutting our conversation short? I bit back my disappointment. It wasn't like he didn't want to talk to me again. He'd asked me to text him tomorrow, for heaven's sake. He was probably going out with friends right now. It was a Friday night, and he wasn't scheduled tomorrow.

I kind of wished he'd asked me to talk about it in person, though. I was dying to see his face while we talked, because I wouldn't have thought in a million years that he was the kind of guy who watched serial killer documentaries. From the conversations we'd had in person, I would've guessed he only watched sports – and while I did enjoy sports, I could only talk about them so much.

But whatever. If he wanted to continue this conversation by text, I'd do it.

Sure, I wrote. *Talk to you later. Enjoy your night.*

Will do, he said. *Hope the movie doesn't keep you up all night.*

I couldn't resist sending one last text. *Keep me up? It's more likely to inspire me!*

*

Working through the weekend was a pain in the ass, especially since Sam didn't have any shifts. Wren kept bugging me for updates, but I didn't have any to give her. "We've been texting" was all I could or would say.

I was quickly getting hooked on bantering with him. We had the same sense of humor, not to mention the same taste in TV shows and music. I found it funny to think I'd once wondered if sports would be the only thing we had to talk about. At this point, it was hard to *stop* talking to him.

By Monday, he still hadn't asked me out. I had today and tomorrow off. Wednesday, we were both on the schedule. I'd finally get to see him again, now that I'd gotten a glimpse of the real him. I couldn't wait to see if our text connection would translate to real life.

I relaxed most of the day, trying not to think too much about Sam. He was probably just waiting to start his new job before he asked me on a date. He must've not wanted things to be messy at work for his last couple of weeks here. Clearly he was interested, or he wouldn't still be texting me. Or could he just be looking for a friend? No, because he'd been so flirtatious when he asked me for my number.

He was also responding to my texts surprisingly quickly considering he was at work. We were always understaffed, and even during the week, I found it hard to get a moment to myself more than once an hour or so. Sam was still replying almost as fast as he had over the weekend, like some kind of texting ninja. I'd have to watch him on Wednesday and try to figure out how he managed to get away from the customers so often.

Of course, I was going to be watching him anyway.

Did Jacob come in today? I texted. Jacob was an older man who came in every morning and sat with his laptop for about five hours. None of the staff knew what he was doing online, and every time somebody asked him, he'd mutter something about hacking into the government.

No, he wrote back after a longer pause than usual. *Guess he had better things to do!*

Better than taking down capitalism? I said. *What could be better than that?*

Hey, even anarchists can have a life, Sam replied. *How do we know he doesn't have a wife and a family?*

It's not too likely, considering that he smells like he showers about once a month.

People are into all sorts of things, he wrote back. *Maybe that turns his wife on!*

At four-thirty, I peeled myself off my bed and padded into the hallway to knock on Chelle's door. "Sure you don't want to come to that meeting?"

She pushed her chair back from her desk. "I wish I could, but there's no time."

"Come on. This is Fronton's first Pride festival we're talking about. You're going to hate yourself forever if you don't help organize it."

"Maybe another time," she said. "I'm in the zone with this essay I'm writing."

She was studying English, after changing her major about a thousand times. Even though she was twenty-three, a year older than me, she had another two years left in college.

"Are you sure?" I asked. "This is, like, a historical event."

"You'll have to go down in history without me," she said. "Sabrina's not going to make it, either. She's giving a guitar lesson."

"Ah, so that's why you're not bothering to come," I teased. "I see how it is. All right, then. I'll let you know how it goes."

"You didn't want me to go, anyway." She put her hands back on the computer keyboard. "I know you. You're going to flirt it up with every pretty girl that's there. I would've just gotten in your way."

"Whoa, now! You act like I'm a player or something."

"Or something." She grinned.

I headed downstairs, still shaking my head. Chelle knew me all too well, but this time she was wrong.

I wasn't going to be flirting with any pretty girls at this Pride meeting. Not when I had a certain boy taking up this much of my mind.

THREE – ELLA

The first Pride festival planning committee meeting was conveniently taking place in one of the boardrooms of the library where I worked. I took off my ID badge and headed over there, fighting the urge to take out my phone. I'd been texting Sam's crush all day, and I was dying to see how she'd respond to my last little joke.

It seemed like Sam had good taste in women. Judi was as cool and smart as he'd said. Even though I had no idea what she looked like, I was developing a tiny bit of a crush on her, myself. Too bad she was into guys – specifically my little brother. Oh, well. If this worked, he could bring her home to meet the family, and I'd make a new friend.

We'd definitely click in real life. I could tell from her quick wit and the things we had in common. In fact, the more I talked to her, the more I wondered why she'd even be interested in Sam. Nothing against him, he was a great guy, but he wasn't exactly deep. Judi, on the other hand… she was extraordinary.

The boardroom was already filled with about ten people, a few of whom I recognized from around town. I said a silent thanks that no girls I'd dated were here. In a town of less than two hundred thousand, the queer community was minuscule, and I'd half-expected an uncomfortable run-in with someone I'd been out with in the past.

I headed over to a guy I vaguely knew named Ian. When he saw me, he squealed and jumped up to give me a hug. "Ella, it's been forever! How have you been? Do you know Julie?" He pointed at the girl on the other side of him.

"No, I don't believe we've met." I looked the girl up and down, trying not to let my jaw drop. I was absolutely certain we hadn't met, actually – I definitely would've remembered her if I'd encountered her before.

She was short and curvy, with fire-engine red hair shaped into a delicate pixie cut. While her features were calm, her eyes were lively. Energy bubbled under her surface, and she gave the impression that she was amused by everything around her.

"Nice to meet you." She took my hand, and a jolt went through my system. "What was your name?"

God, I'd forgotten to even introduce myself. "Ella."

A smile turned her lips upward, and she bit the lower one as if trying – unsuccessfully – to stop it. "How do you know Ian?"

"We went to college together," Ian said before I could get a word in. "We both volunteered at the LGBT club, but Ella was getting her master's in library science while I was wasting my time on that damn accounting degree."

"Did you not find a job yet?" I asked.

I only half-paid attention to the answer. I wanted to sit closer to Julie, to ask her more about herself. Ian had planted himself directly between us, blocking her completely from my view. I leaned forward so I could see her, hoping I came off like I wanted to involve her in the conversation. She met my eyes, and the way she held my gaze told me she knew exactly what I was doing.

"So it's really that tough to find an accounting gig out here?" she asked, appearing completely unruffled even though she was still keeping her eyes on me. "Have you thought about moving back out to Denver?"

"I've thought about it, but I don't see how it could work," Ian said. "I don't have the money to move out there and start paying rent while I job-hunt. Life was so much better out there while we were in college, though, wasn't it?" He nudged me.

"I don't know," I said. "I like Fronton."

I wanted to ask Julie what she did for a living, but Ian launched into a speech on the comparative merits of Fronton versus Denver. Apparently Denver was better in terms of the queer community, the education, the nightlife, and the culture, and Fronton had no benefits whatsoever.

"Denver isn't so great," Julie said. "It's so crowded, traffic is terrible, and housing prices are getting out of hand."

"Sounds like you know the city pretty well," I said, desperate to learn more about her.

She nodded, and Ian cut her off again. "Sure, it's not perfect, but it's a whole lot better than this hellhole. Fronton is like the gaping asshole of Colorado."

The whole table had gone quiet as he said that, and the rest of the planning committee gaped at him. I stifled a laugh, and although he was still partly blocking my view of her, I caught a glimpse of Julie doing the same.

"Um, okay. Let's call this meeting to order," a tall guy said, standing up at the head of the table. "My name is Todd, and as you all know, we're going to be organizing the first-ever Pride festival for… the gaping asshole of Colorado."

I choked on nothing, and Ian patted my back with a smirk. I would've felt better about the profanity if everyone here was around our age, but there was a gay couple who looked to be in their fifties on the other side of the table, and an androgynous person who seemed to be a teenager a few seats past Julie. Luckily, all of them were laughing.

"Where do we start?" someone asked.

"When's it happening?" someone else put in.

"If someone wants to join the committee later, is

that okay?" Julie asked.

Todd held up his hands. "I'm going to tell you a bit about what we have planned so far, and then you can ask your questions – one at a time."

I settled back in my seat and listened. Apparently the festival was going to take place in mid-June. Todd was going to form us into subcommittees so that all of the necessary duties would get done. And other people, including Julie's roommate, were welcome to join in at any time.

By the end of the meeting, I was feeling good about the festival's potential. Even though it was the first year and none of us had organized anything like this before, we had a room full of people who were excited and passionate about making it happen. There was a lot to get done before mid-June, but with all of us working together, I was sure we could pull it off.

I was on the fundraising subcommittee, so I'd be trying to find corporate sponsors and helping to plan a fundraising event. Ian and Julie were on the marketing subcommittee, which meant they'd be putting posters up all over Fronton and trying to get the word about the festival. Their job seemed like more fun than mine – or maybe I was just disappointed because I hadn't been placed with Julie.

"Thanks again for coming," Todd said. "I'm looking forward to seeing all of you in two weeks. Same place, same time."

Everyone filed out, chatting about their ideas for the festival. Even though Fronton was a small town, having a Pride event was going to be a big deal for the people who lived here. I imagined the older generation would've never guessed such a thing would ever happen in their own town.

Ian, Julie, and I walked out of the library and paused to say our goodbyes. "I have to head home," Ian said. "See you next time?"

"Of course," I said. "Great running into you." I hoped seeing each other more often might turn him from an acquaintance into a friend. He was a cool guy – when he wasn't getting between me and a pretty girl.

"Good to see you," Julie said, giving him a big hug.

As he headed for his car, Julie turned to face me with another amused smile. Could she tell how nervous I was right now? I'd been hoping to get her alone since I'd met her, and now that it was finally happening, I couldn't even look her in the eye.

"Well, I'd better get going," she said.

I couldn't just let her leave like that. It was so rare to meet a cute lesbian here in Fronton, and even if we'd barely spoken, I'd seen enough of her to know I was interested. Maybe she felt the same way. I'd never know if I didn't take a chance.

"Do – do you have plans?" I stuttered out, staring at her black combat boots. "Right now, I mean? I was thinking about grabbing a coffee, so if you wanted to get one with me…"

She hesitated long enough that I looked her in the eyes again – her very pretty, deep blue eyes. "Sorry if it's awkward to be so upfront, but are you asking me on a coffee date?"

"Um… I guess, yeah. You could put it like that." *Way to exude confidence, Ella.*

Her smile turned regretful. "I have to say I'm flattered," she said. "If things were different, I would've loved to."

"Oh, God. You're seeing someone."

"Not even!" she quickly said. "There's just someone that I'm interested in. Too interested, really. I'm crushing hard, and it wouldn't be fair to you to act like I'm totally single when my mind's actually on someone else."

I bit my lip. "Oh."

"Thank you, though! Really." She twirled a piece of bright red hair around a finger. "If it weren't for that, I would've gone in a heartbeat. You're adorable."

Adorable? Not really what I was going for. But still, she was clearly making an effort to make her rejection as gentle as possible, and I had to be gracious about it. "No problem," I said. "You're gorgeous, obviously, but you seem like a cool, fun person as well. I hope this won't make things weird, since we're going to be volunteering together. Maybe we can still be friends."

"Friends sounds good." She licked her pillowy lips. "I'll see you around, then, Ella."

"See you."

I stared after her as she walked away. Her crush was one lucky lady. They'd probably be a couple soon.

Who could turn down someone like that?

FOUR – JUDI

I placed the tray of bagels inside the display case. The door chimed, and I stood so quickly I banged my head on the top of the case. "Ow!" I said to myself, rubbing the back of my skull. I turned to the entrance. "It's you?"

Wren smirked at me. "Hoping for lover-boy, huh?"

I hadn't meant to sound so disappointed. "Not at all, but... isn't Sam working today?"

"Yeah, he is. I just swung by to grab one of those." She pointed at the sprinkle donuts.

"At seven a.m.?"

"It's for later. I'm going on a road trip, and I didn't want to go a full day without my fix."

I put the donut in a bag and waved away her money when she tried to pay for it. "Don't be silly. And have fun."

"I plan to. And..." Her eyes slid to the door as it chimed again. "You too."

Sam walked in, and my heart jumped. He looked as cute as ever, even with his hair wet from the snow. I gave him a little wave. After all the texting we'd been doing, I felt oddly shy to talk to him in person.

"Hey," he said casually, as if he hadn't been

texting me nonstop until we both fell asleep last night. "How's it going?"

"Not bad." My cheeks were already getting hot. "How about you?"

"I'm good. Give me a sec." He squeezed by me to get to the back room.

"I'll leave you lovebirds to it," Wren said.

"We're not lovebirds!" I whispered furiously. "Nothing has even happened! He hasn't asked me out."

"Why don't you ask him?"

It was a good question. If he'd been a girl, I wouldn't have hesitated. When it was two girls, gender roles didn't apply. Somebody had to make the first move, or nothing would ever happen. With a guy, it was different. As much as they said they liked a confident woman, I knew a lot of men were turned off when a girl took the lead.

I'd never been able to understand why that was the case. Personally, I adored when a woman had the courage to make their interest known. Like that girl on the weekend, Ella. She was cute as a button – even if she probably wouldn't describe herself that way.

She seemed to be trying to look like a "real" librarian, with her short dark hair and thick-rimmed glasses. But she was tall and a little gawky, and her youthful features gave away that she must've only finished her masters a year or two ago.

I'd felt her interest from the moment we met, although I hadn't expected her to act on it so quickly. Her asking me out was a pleasant surprise, and I'd hated having to turn it down. She'd taken it well, though, and who knew? If things didn't work out with Sam, maybe something could happen there. Clearly we had some chemistry.

But I hoped things would work out with Sam. I'd been thinking about him constantly since we'd started to text. Our interests were way more similar than I'd ever thought, and our personalities completely aligned. I just wondered if he'd let that side of himself show in person now that I'd seen it over text.

"I don't want to scare him off by asking him out," I said. "Besides, I think he might be waiting until he leaves this job. I'll wait and see what happens then."

"Whatever you say," Wren said. "Here he comes!"

She made a silent exit as Sam came toward me. I gave him a nervous smile, getting ready to say something about the song he'd recommended to me last night. Before I could speak, the door chimed once more and our first customer of the day walked in. Just my luck, the woman wanted a fancy steamed-milk latte that was going to take a minute to make. And another customer was already coming in behind her.

The morning was so busy that I only got to talk to Sam as much as I normally did. We exchanged a few glances, and made the odd comment towards each other, but there was no time for an actual conversation.

"All right, I'm going to take my break," I said at eleven. "I'm going to listen to the rest of the album from that band you told me about, by the way. I downloaded the whole thing."

He dropped fruit into the blender to make a smoothie. "Band?"

"You know – "

He pressed the blend button, and the sound drowned out what I'd been about to say.

Shrugging, I headed into the back room and put my headphones on. The band, Luscious Karma, made an eclectic blend of folk music and indie pop. I'd been listening to the song he'd recommended on repeat all night, and if the rest of the album was like that, they'd soon become a new favorite.

Out of habit, I checked my phone for new messages. It was silly, since the person I wanted to hear from was right out there – I'd been next to him all morning. But somehow, even though he was physically present, I felt like he wasn't there at all.

Oddly enough, I did have a new text from him. *Morning! Did you listen to any more of Luscious Karma's songs?* He'd sent it half an hour ago.

Frowning, I heaved myself onto my aching feet. There were no customers in line, for once, so I held up my phone. "When did you have time to text me this?"

He blinked, then grinned. "I'm talented."

So he was being shy? "It's cute that you want to text me while I'm right here, but… you know you could just talk to me in person, right?"

"I know that."

"And to answer your question, I was listening to more of their songs during my break." I still had a few minutes left, but I looped my apron back around my neck anyway. "I really like 'Set A Fire.'"

"Oh yeah, that one's really good." He scratched the back of his neck and rubbed a cloth over the counter, even though it already looked clean.

I stepped closer, wanting to make the most of this moment before more customers came in. "What's your favorite of their songs? Other than the one you sent me, of course."

"Um… I love them all. I couldn't pick a favorite."

"But if you were to choose one?" I pressed.

"I couldn't." He tossed the cloth to the side. "I've actually been listening to Raw Dog a lot lately."

"Raw Dog, the rapper who just got out of jail for assaulting his girlfriend?"

He nodded brightly. "He was already good before he went to jail, and his new album is even better. The beats on the first single are dope!"

Fucking meathead. He didn't even care that Raw Dog had laid hands on a woman? I'd seen the pictures of her online, her face bruised and bloodied. No matter how good someone's music was, I wouldn't support them if they did things like that. I *couldn't,* and I didn't want to date someone who would, either.

"I'm surprised," I said, trying to hide my disgust. "I thought you were more into folk music, indie…"

He blinked rapidly. "I like all kinds of music, actually."

A customer approached the counter, and I turned toward her. Sam took his apron off, mouthing something about taking his break. I wished we'd been able to talk a bit longer. The lunch rush would start soon, which meant we wouldn't have another moment to ourselves for hours.

Could it be that we vibed better over text than in person? My friends who had tried online dating had told me that some people had a different persona when they communicated through the written word. I wouldn't have thought that could happen with Sam since we already knew each other, but it seemed like it had to be something like that.

All of the playfulness we'd built up over the

past few days was gone. He hadn't referred once to our little jokes or hit me with any mild teasing. He was acting the exact same as he had before he'd ever texted me.

Or... could it be *me* who was different over text? Had I felt more comfortable with him when I wasn't looking at him face-to-face? Now that I thought about it, I hadn't acted any friendlier than usual with him this morning. I'd been so nervous to see him, I'd probably come across a bit standoffish. I'd try to do better when we had another chance to talk.

The fact that he liked Raw Dog was a turn-off, but not an immediate dealbreaker. Straight white men weren't exactly known for being into social justice. Maybe he'd never thought about the implications of listening to an abuser's music. It was worth having a conversation about it. I'd see if he was open to changing his views.

The real test would be how he reacted when I told him I was bisexual. A lot of straight guys took it to mean I was some kind of kinky sex addict who would give him all the threesomes he wanted. I kind of expected Sam to be like that, which was probably why I was putting off telling him. I needed to bite the bullet and do it, and let his reaction tell me what to do next.

I worked assiduously through the lunch rush, only speaking to Sam when it was necessary. Once things slowed down a little, I looked over at him again.

"What are your plans for the rest of the week?" I asked. "I mean, other than work and watching creepy documentaries."

He frowned slightly. "Not too much, I guess. I'm scheduled every day until Friday."

"I feel you. I'm working every day through the weekend." The other days were busier, so Wren or our other coworkers would be here. We wouldn't be alone again until next Wednesday.

"I'm going to watch the football game with some buddies tomorrow, and that's about it, in terms of fun."

"Oh, yeah. The Broncos are playing the Cowboys, right?"

His eyes lit up. "You know your stuff." He hesitated. "I'd invite you, but it's going to be a bunch of bros. I don't know if it'd be fun for you."

"I definitely want our first date to be more romantic than that."

Now his whole face lit up. "I agree. Um… maybe we could go watch a game at Shady's on Sunday night."

The local sports bar? That wasn't too romantic, either. I'd thought he might want to go see an interesting movie, or even drive to Denver to see a show. We had so much more in common than sports.

He must've seen the distaste on my face. "Or we

could go to dinner."

"Great!"

"Do you like burgers?"

For a first date, not really... But if I said that, I'd sound too picky. I *wanted* to go out with this guy. Why would it matter where we ate? I forced myself to nod. "Sounds like a plan."

"Cool." He rearranged a stack of coffee cups. "I'm looking forward to it."

"Me, too." Leaning on the counter, I watched him move. "You know, you're really different over text than in person."

He froze. "Am I?"

"Mm-hmm. Very different."

He gave me a weak smile. "Well, I hope you like me better in real life."

Five – Ella

I lay on the couch, wrapped up in a heated blanket, the latest psychological thriller from my favorite author in my hands. People thought librarians sat around reading all day, which was the furthest thing from the truth. My work kept me occupied from nine to five. On top of that, I'd been calling different companies every day, looking for sponsors for the Pride festival. I only had time to relax with this book right now because Sam was doing my chores for the week.

The plot was just beginning to get juicy. The narrator's daughter had disappeared, and then her husband had vanished as well. I'd thought he was the bad guy, but now it was becoming clear that she was an unreliable narrator, and it seemed like maybe she'd kidnapped the daughter herself. I licked my finger and turned the page, silently thanking Sam for allowing me this free time.

"Ella!"

Speak of the devil. Sam had just stepped into the room, and he looked furious.

I lowered the book by an inch and pushed up my glasses. "Just a second. I'm in the middle of the chapter."

"Put the book down," he growled. "What

exactly have you been saying to Judi?"

Reluctantly, I set the book, open to the page I'd been reading, across my chest. "Nothing in particular," I said. "Just chatting."

I'd actually forgotten Sam was going to see her in person today, and I'd texted her like usual. Sometimes when we texted, I forgot he had anything to do with her. Talking to her felt like talking to a friend, albeit one I hadn't met.

"You were supposed to get me a date!" he said, throwing up his hands. "Now she thinks I'm a whole different person. She thinks I'm into *folk music,* for heaven's sake. And *documentaries.*"

"Well…" I sat up slowly, pushing the blanket aside. "I thought you wanted her to like you."

"Yeah, to like *me,*" he said. "I thought you were going to pretend to be me. Like, a cooler, more suave version of me. You made me into *you* instead!"

I bit my lip. I was starting to think I'd fucked up. "I was trying to bond over things we have in common."

"And now she thinks I have them in common with her!" He shook his head, pacing around the room. "What am I supposed to do? I can't tell her she was talking to somebody else. I'm going to have to pretend I like folk music until the day I die. Folk music!"

"You're being dramatic. You're not going to marry this girl."

"I could've!" he said. "I told you, I really like her. I thought this could be something serious, but it's not going to be if you start off by lying to her about who I am."

"Hey, don't blame me. You asked me to do this."

"I asked you to make me look good, not to make me into someone else entirely!"

I rubbed my temples. "Okay, clearly we had a misunderstanding. We can fix this."

"Let me see the messages you sent her."

Nervously, I handed him his phone. He'd lent it to me for the duration of the Judi Project, and had installed texting apps on his tablet so he could keep in touch with his friends.

He looked from the screen to me, and then back. His eyes bugged out more and more as he read through the conversation.

"You've been texting her nonstop since I gave you her number!" he said, still scrolling up. "Oh my God, it doesn't end."

"Is that so bad?" I asked in a small voice. "I thought I was bonding with her for you."

"More like for yourself," he said. "I don't even know anything about half the stuff you two talked about!"

"You wanted me to make you sound smart."

"By throwing a big word in here and there!" he said. "Not by talking about the inevitable downfall of civilization! How am I supposed to talk about this on a date?"

"That's it!" I said. "I'll ask her for a date. Then you can meet with her in person and just be yourself. You can win her over in your own way."

"She already agreed to a date," he said unhappily. "I asked her in person."

"Then my work is done!" I said. "That's what you wanted… isn't it?"

"No!" He waved the phone at me. "She's expecting *this* person to show up, not me." He sank into the armchair. "What am I going to do?"

I didn't know what to tell him.

After a minute, Coco appeared in the doorway. "Sam, I'm hungry," she said. "Are you making dinner?"

"Yeah, I was about to get started." He stood up, then paused. "You know what? I think it's Ella's turn to cook tonight."

I'd messed up my end of our deal. I couldn't expect him to keep his anymore. "Right," I said, regretfully setting my book on the coffee table. "I was about to get started."

*

Sam and I stayed off the topic of Judi throughout dinner. Instead, we talked about Coco's science fair project and the new car Mom was thinking of getting.

The spaghetti I'd attempted to make was chewy and undercooked, and I knew from the way everyone kept reaching for water that I'd added too much salt. I wasn't as good a cook as Mom or Sam, but tonight was bad even for me.

Once we were finished eating, I cleared the table and washed the dishes. Sam hovered at the edge of the room as if waiting for Mom and Coco to leave.

When they were gone, he came over to me. "I figured out the answer," he said, his eyes bright, his voice nearly a whisper.

"How you can win Judi over? Do tell." I shut the tap off and turned toward him, crossing my arms.

"You're going to help me," he said. "I'll call you, and then I'll put my phone in my lap. You'll be able to hear our whole conversation, and you'll text me what I should say."

I raised my eyebrows. "There's no way this could go wrong."

"I know! It's such a good plan."

"Sam, I was being sarcastic." I rolled my eyes. "It's a terrible plan! How would that even work without her noticing? And more importantly, how's she going to fall for you yourself when you'd still be using my words?" I paused. "Are you even trying to get her to fall for her, or do you just want to get in her pants?"

"It's not about sex!" he said defensively. "I just need your help to get things started. Now that you messed up the texting, I have to pretend to be the person you made me sound like. Then I can be a little more myself on the second date, and a little more, until finally I'm just me."

"Why would she want to keep dating you at that point?" I asked. "Once she realizes you're not the guy she fell for, won't she break things off?"

He looked worried for a second, then grinned. "Nah. By then, she'll be stuck with me."

"This is a terrible plan," I said again. "Why don't you just tell her you were trying to impress her and you lied about being into some things you're not actually into? Or, you know… be honest, and tell her you had your sister text her for a few days?"

"Tell her I lied to her? That's no way to start a relationship."

I shook my head. "I'm not going to do this, Sam. I'm not going to trick some poor girl into a relationship with you. If she doesn't like you for you, you two aren't meant to be." I headed toward the door of the kitchen.

Sam's voice stopped me. "I'll do your chores for another week."

I paused. "Two weeks total?"

"Yeah. One night of helping me for one week of chores. It'll be a win-win – for everyone." He gestured at the stove. "All of us will benefit from not having to eat your cooking."

I scoffed. My cooking was fine – usually. But... "All of my other chores, too?"

"Sure."

"Even if I don't get you a second date?"

"You better." He glared at me. "But yeah. One week of chores, no matter what the night's outcome is."

I thought longingly of the thriller I'd been reading. I could get through so many more books with another week of freedom from chores.

Was it wrong? I'd be tricking this girl... but on the other hand, I didn't even know her.

"Fine, I'll do it," I muttered.

What was the worst that could happen?

Six – Judi

The plan was to meet at Belly Burger tonight at six. I finished work at four and rushed home to get changed. I wanted to look nice for this date, even if I was back to being on the fence about Sam.

Working with him on Thursday and Friday had felt like it did before I gave him my number. It didn't feel like our text conversations had brought us any closer. If anything, he'd seemed more distant. It was as if he was embarrassed about showing me his true self, and had decided to pull away again.

He'd been texting me after work, but not like before. His responses were slower, and he was less enthusiastic. I almost wondered if he was losing interest in me. If he'd met somebody else he liked more.

Flopping down onto my bed, I scrolled through our last few messages.

Enjoying your weekend off? I'd texted. *You're so lucky you're not at work right now. We're slammed and it's C-R-A-Z-Y!*

That's a pretty long text for someone who's slammed, he'd written back half an hour later. *Seems like it must not be that busy if you're still on your phone!*

I'd texted that on my break, so I hadn't seen his

message until later. *Phew,* I'd written then. *Just got off. See you at 6?*

Right! Looking forward to it.

It was a fine exchange, just... dull. If he hadn't been so interesting before, I wouldn't have minded. But a few days ago, he'd always responded near-instantly and our conversation topics had ranged from criminal psychology to space exploration and animal rights. He'd made my expectations go up, and now I wanted more than "fine" from him.

But we'd get to that point again. I just needed to get him to share that side of himself with me. It was in there somewhere, or he wouldn't have chatted with me like that. The only question was how to bring it out of him. If it was a matter of being comfortable with me, the only solution might be to give him time.

I got up and peeked into my closet. I pulled out a couple of sweater-dresses and laid them across the bed. I wanted to look casual, yet cute and feminine.

Much of my closet space was taken up by more boyish clothes. I tended to have a bit of a tomboy vibe, but I liked being able to femme it up when I felt like it as well. I'd often asked myself if I might be nonbinary or genderfluid – those identity questions had come up a lot during my major in gender studies. In the end, I'd decided I could be female and be a little boyish as well.

I threw on a navy-blue dress, combed my hair, and applied some light make-up. It was time.

I arrived at the restaurant a minute before six. To my pleasant surprise, it was decently upscale for a burger joint. It was a sit-down restaurant, and the menu in the window showed they even had options other than burgers.

"Hey!" Sam's voice came from a nearby table, and he stood up to clasp me in a quick hug. "I got us a table already."

"And here I thought I was early." I looked him up and down, appreciating the checkered button-down shirt he'd worn. It seemed like he'd made a little extra effort to look nice for me, too.

"I guess I was keen," he said, pulling out my chair for me. "Have you been here before? It's one of my favorite spots, so I can recommend something if you'd like."

"Sure! I'm actually not huge on burgers, so I wouldn't mind trying something from the wrap section." I pointed at the menu.

He cringed. "Oh God, you're not a vegetarian or something, are you?"

"Not at all. Don't worry." The poor guy seemed so nervous, I patted his hand to set him at ease. "I don't eat a ton of meat, especially red meat, but that's just because I don't like it. Plus, vegetables are delicious."

"Vegetables are disgusting." He jerked as if

taken by surprise, then looked down at his lap. "I mean, I do like some vegetables, though. Like carrots – who could say no to a raw carrot, right?"

"Totally. It's the perfect snack."

He rested his chin in his hand, looking down again. "Hey, do you think a tomato is a fruit or a vegetable?"

"Fruit, definitely."

"But it goes in salads with all the other vegetables. And every other fruit is sweet, so like, how could it be a real fruit?"

"That's the thing, not every fruit is sweet," I said. "Did you know avocados are technically fruits?"

"Really?"

I nodded. "They're botanically classified as a berry."

I leaned forward, engaged in the conversation. This felt almost like those early texts again. The topic was interesting, and we were vibing. I wondered what witty remark he'd make in response.

He blinked at me. "You're so smart."

I shook my head, suddenly uncomfortable. Over text, he never would've said something like that. He would've had some smart response. Maybe he was one of those people who always thought of the right thing to say too late. Then again, he was always quick with his text replies – so what was the issue now?

The waiter came by to take our order, and at Sam's urging, I decided on a chicken Caesar wrap. He got an everything burger.

Once the waiter left, Sam looked down again. It was an odd tic I'd never noticed at work. I guessed he was more nervous than usual since we were out on an official date.

"How was work?" he asked. "Did any of our favorites come in?"

"Jacob was his usual self," I said with a laugh. "One of these days he'll manage to hack the government. God only knows what he'll do once he gets in."

"Ah. Um…" He looked down. "You never know. He might do better than the current administration."

"True, maybe he has a plan to revolutionize healthcare."

Sam squirmed, looking uncomfortable. I could've kicked myself for mentioning politics. This was a first date, after all.

"What did you get up to today?" I asked. "Did you watch anything good?"

He visibly relaxed. "I watched the replay of the Heat game from last night. Did you catch it?"

"No, I was working. I'm not a huge fan of the Heat, anyway."

He frowned. "I thought you were into basketball."

"Yeah, I like it, but I don't watch every game."

The waiter brought our food, and we were quiet for a moment as we dug in. My wrap tasted good at first, but after a few bites, the flavors merged and the whole thing became kind of boring. A little bit like Sam.

He set down his burger and looked at his lap again. "I feel like I don't know that much about your past. Did you grow up around here?"

His arm had moved before he said that, almost as if... As if he was looking at his phone.

My jaw slowly dropped open as I stared at him. Had I just figured the Sam mystery out? Had he been Googling what to say to me the whole time we'd been texting? Had he been looking for conversation topics on the Internet all night?

"Um... I..." I shook my head, mentally debating whether I should confront him about what he was doing. On the one hand, it was weird and awkward. On the other hand, was there even a point? Clearly he was trying a bit too hard because he liked me, so calling him out would only embarrass him. I was pretty sure I wasn't interested anymore, but pointing out his behavior would be borderline cruel.

I'd finish my meal, then cut the date short.

"I did grow up locally," I said, forcing a smile. "On the other side of town, though. I went to college in Denver, and then I came back."

"Me, too," he said. "I thought about staying there, but I have all my old friends here, and I'm really close with my family."

"Oh yes, your snowball fight competitors," I said. "How many brothers and sisters do you have?"

"Two sisters. One older, one younger. They're…" He shook his head. "They're great, generally."

"That's great. I'm an only child. I always wondered what it'd be like to have siblings."

He looked down and frowned. "I feel like having sisters has made me understand the female perspective a little more than the average guy," he said, still not meeting my eyes. "It's turned me into a sensitive kind of person."

Was he even serious? He sounded so cheesy right now, and from the look on his face, he could barely stand to force the words out.

I crammed the last bit of my wrap into my mouth. He was still eating, though, and his drink was only half-gone. I settled back in my seat, trying not to sigh. A few more minutes, and this would be over.

We made more small talk as he finished his burger. Now that I'd noticed the phone thing, it was hard to see how I'd ever missed it. Of course he didn't have a tic, for heaven's sake. The only thing I didn't get was how he didn't notice me rolling my eyes whenever he looked at his lap.

At last, his plate held nothing but crumbs. Still, he made no move to drain his Coke. I fidgeted in my seat, eager to leave. How long was he going to drag this out?

After another minute of chit-chat, I'd had enough of being polite. "Well, this was fun, but I have to get going," I said, making a show of looking at my watch. "I have plans with a friend." A friend named Netflix.

"Oh… already?" he asked, looking concerned. "I didn't realize, or I would've picked another day. I thought tonight would be good, since tomorrow's your day off."

"That was nice of you." I pulled my wallet out of my purse, determined to not let him pay for me. "You're scheduled tomorrow, though. I'm sure you don't want to be out too late."

"I don't mind. I…" He paused and checked his phone. "But you have to go, so it's fine. No worries."

He gestured the waiter over, and once we'd paid, we stood up. Outside, I braced myself for our goodbye. "This was great," he said. "Maybe we can do it again sometime."

He went in for a hug, which I reluctantly returned. *Don't try to kiss me. Don't try to kiss me.* I pre-emptively turned my face away.

"We'll talk about it," I said, quickly stepping

away. "Text me!"

I probably should've told him there wouldn't be a second date. It just felt unnecessarily cruel to reject him to his face.

At least we only had a few more days of working together. After the end of this week, I wouldn't have to see him at Caffeine Hut anymore.

There was no chance in hell I'd go out with him again.

Seven – Ella

Sam got home about twenty minutes after Judi said goodbye. By then, I was on the living room couch with Coco, watching the end of *Tizzy's Magical Adventures*. I'd given up my own Sunday evening plans to sit in my room, listening to Sam's date on speakerphone and rapidly typing out whatever I thought he should say.

"Thank you, Ella!" he said, dropping onto the couch between me and Coco and leaning his head on my shoulder. "That went amazingly!"

"Really?" The conversation hadn't flowed particularly well, if you asked me. Judi hadn't flirted at all, and then she'd left immediately after dinner. It didn't bode well for Sam's chances of a second date.

"It was so good," he enthused. "She's so great. She's perfect for me."

"What?" Coco asked, pausing the DVD. "Who?"

"Nobody," I said. "I think it's your bedtime, actually."

"But Ella!"

"But nothing." I grabbed the remote and flipped off the TV. "The grown-ups need to talk. You can finish watching tomorrow."

She groaned so loudly I would've felt bad if I hadn't known she'd seen the movie a hundred thousand times before. I wasn't exactly preventing her from finding out the ending.

Once she was gone, I turned to Sam. "You're really that into her?"

To me, it'd sounded like the best parts of the conversation were when he repeated the things I told him. When he talked about things he was interested in – which I'd encouraged him to do, since he did want to just be himself eventually – I could practically hear Judi's interest evaporating.

She seemed like such a cool person. Even without knowing what she looked like, I knew we had more than enough in common to be friends, if not more. And Sam, as wonderful as he was, didn't share those interests. Honestly, I wasn't sure why he was so enthralled by her.

"She's amazing," he said, lying down across the couch and sticking his legs over my lap. "She's just so smart, you know? And she's cool, and confident, and… ugh!"

Couldn't he see that a smart girl might want to be with someone who was smart, too? I was going to have to break this to him gently, but I didn't quite know how.

"She didn't say she wanted a second date," I said carefully. "Are you sure she had a good time?"

"Yeah, I think so." He looked confused. "She said I should text her. I'll probably ask her in person, actually. We can plan it out at work."

"Well… are you sure you'll be ready for a second date?" I asked. "Without me helping you, I mean?"

He sat up straight. "Um… maybe you could help me again."

"You said this was a one-time thing!" I said. "You said if you got to a second date, you'd be yourself!"

"I can't do that."

"Of course you can. How did you expect to keep this situation going forever? Am I supposed to stay on the phone while you're in bed with her?" I wrinkled my nose at the thought.

"I don't know," he said. "I can't do this on my own yet, though. At least keep texting her for me. Just for a little longer."

I sighed. "I can text her, but it's not going to work for much longer. If you guys go on more dates, I won't know what you talked about. It'll be obvious that someone else is texting her."

"That's why you should stay on the phone during those dates, too." He flashed me a smile.

My little brother thought his puppy-dog eyes would get him whatever he wanted. Well, I had a feeling Judi wouldn't agree to any more dates, anyway. "I guess I can text her for now," I said.

"Then we'll see how things go."

I had another, more selfish reason to agree to text her. It was, simply put, fun. Even though I hadn't met her, I enjoyed talking to her more than I did to most people in my life. I'd come to see her as something like a text buddy. Chatting with her made my days more pleasant.

I'd pulled back somewhat when Sam had yelled at me, and I'd done my best to sound more like him, like he'd asked. But I was still myself, and I knew my own voice, thoughts, and opinions came through.

I was going to miss her when Sam took his phone back. I wished there was a way to keep our text conversation going – or to meet and befriend her in person instead. It might've been silly, since we'd only communicated through words on a screen… but I felt like I'd really connected with her. A genuine human connection was hard to find, and I didn't want to give it up.

"Great!" Sam said. "Keep my phone. Text her in the morning."

"That soon?"

"Or whenever you feel is good," he said. "You're the expert, after all."

*

I tried to keep the conversation with Judi going over the next few days. I could feel her pulling away, though. Her replies were slower, and there was less flirting and teasing. I was pretty sure she was building up to telling Sam she wasn't interested.

I wish I didn't have to go to work tomorrow, she texted on Tuesday. *I'm so over this job thing. Can I retire already?*

I'm with you! I wrote, sitting behind the front desk at the library. *Let's give up our material possessions, move to a farm in the countryside, and live off the land for the rest of our lives.*

Yeah, right. You already have your fancy new job that's going to be a million times better than Caffeine Hut.

I put my phone down to help a patron who was looking for a book. I didn't mind my job at all, actually, but I couldn't tell Judi that.

My new job will have its own issues, I wrote back when I was done. *Every job does. Besides, I'm opposed to the whole concept of work. Money can't buy you happiness!*

But it can buy you food and shelter, she said. *I don't think I'd be too happy without those.*

I told you, we'll live off the land together. I considered adding a winky face, then decided against it. If she was planning to reject Sam soon, I didn't want to freak her out by coming on too strong.

I skimmed through a library newsletter while I waited for her response. I had to make some acquisitions soon, which was one of my favorite parts of the job. But I wouldn't be able to focus on picking out new books I thought the library patrons would enjoy while I had my mind on Judi.

I didn't know you felt so strongly about work, she said. *Even if you could have your dream job, you'd rather not work at all?*

Oops. I'd come to realize that when she said she didn't know something about me, that meant I'd strayed too far from sounding like Sam.

Nah, I'm kind of joking, I typed. *I mean, living off the land would be a ton of work, too. I just feel like it'd be more enjoyable than Caffeine Hut.*

Maybe so, she said. *Just about anything would be more enjoyable than Caffeine Hut.*

That could've been another good moment to flirt. I considered saying something like "it must be so much worse without me there," but again decided against it.

If I didn't push her to be more than friends, maybe she and "Sam" could keep texting after he left his job. They could keep in touch over the phone – they wouldn't have to see each other. Of course, I'd have to give him his phone back at some point. Maybe I could give her my number and tell her it was Sam's new number.

What would be your dream job, then? I texted.

Hmm, I'm not sure. Not much you can do with a degree in gender studies, you know?

My eyes nearly popped out of my head. She'd taken gender studies? That was one of the gayest majors out there. I guessed some straight girls studied it, but they had to be few and far between. Was Judi one of them? Or was she not as straight as I'd always imagined?

Another text from her arrived. *I've always thought librarians had a pretty sweet gig, though.*

My eyes got even bigger, and I covered my mouth to hide my dropped jaw. She wanted to be a librarian? I could tell her all about it – the positives, the negatives, the job market. But not while I was still pretending to be Sam.

Unless… *Have I mentioned my sister's a librarian?* I typed carefully. *If you have any questions about the job, I can ask her.*

What if I told her I could put her in touch with "my sister" – that they should meet for a coffee and talk about librarianship as a potential career? I'd get to meet Judi – in person – as myself. The idea was thrilling enough to make my heart beat a little faster, and I glanced around the library as if someone might catch me doing something wrong.

It was much too early to offer anything like that, of course. I didn't even know if Judi had seriously considered becoming a librarian, or if it was just a random thought. I'd have to wait and see how she responded to that last text. But what if... what if...

My phone vibrated on my lap. She was replying faster again, seeming to relax as we fell back into our texting routine. *That's sweet of you!* she said. *I'll have to think about what I'd want to know. I never thought too much about it. Just always thought it'd be cool to be surrounded by books.*

I sighed. So much for meeting up. *My sister says it's not as relaxing as you might think,* I wrote. *There are a lot of different issues she has to deal with. And it's tough to find a job. She was so lucky to find one here in town.*

I see what you mean. I should've figured there'd be more to it than I thought. She added a smiley face. *What about you, anyway? What'd be your dream job?*

I stared at the screen, letting out a slow exhale. Personally, I was already on track for my dream job – being a senior librarian. But she wasn't asking me.

How would Sam answer this question? I wasn't sure, and I didn't want to think about it.

The longer I talked to Judi, the more I hated pretending to be somebody other than me.

EIGHT – JUDI

On Friday, I rushed from work to the library downtown where the Pride planning meeting was taking place. As I walked in, I glanced around the peaceful environment. My chat with Sam the other day had put the idea of becoming a librarian in my head again. It'd always been my dream when I was little, and then I'd put it aside as I got older.

It seemed like a nice, quiet job for someone like me. Library patrons couldn't be nearly as annoying as coffee shop patrons, and I wouldn't have to be on my feet all day. Plus I adored the smell of books. On the other hand, Sam was probably right about the job market. Libraries were getting defunded all over the country, thanks to the rise of the Internet as well as political issues, and I didn't want to go into a dying field.

I wondered if one of the librarians behind the desk might be Sam's sister. Not that it mattered, since I wouldn't be meeting his family anytime soon. We'd gone back to texting like normal after our not-so-great date. We'd gotten along so well over text, I'd started to think about giving him another shot. Then the last couple days at work had been just as bad as the date.

I was ready to accept that we just got along

better over text than in person. If I was right about him Googling things to talk about, that probably had something to do with it. In any case, he'd asked me in person for a second date, and I'd said I was busy. I hoped he could take a hint. If not, I'd reject him properly.

The Pride meeting was already getting started when I slipped into the boardroom. I took a seat next to Ian, and peeked around him to say hi to Ella, the pretty girl who'd asked me out last time. I hadn't thought much about her since two weeks ago. We'd barely interacted, and I didn't know much about her. Now I looked at her with renewed interest. If I wasn't going to go for Sam, maybe I could try getting coffee with her. But I'd want to get to know her a little first.

The group spent a few minutes talking about the overall status of things, and then each subcommittee's head updated us on what they'd accomplished since the last meeting. I panicked for a second, until I remembered Ian had been in charge of designing the posters for us. I hadn't had to do anything over the past two weeks.

He pulled out a few sheets of paper when it came to his turn. "I made a few versions," he said, sounding uncharacteristically shy as he passed them around. "Go easy on me, okay?"

I peered at the different designs. One had the rainbow colors painted over the whole page, while another had blocks of color. One said "2019 Pride Festival" and hardly anything else, and another was full of information.

I looked back and forth between them. Each was better than the last. I had no idea how I'd even begin to decide between them, and the whole subcommittee was going to have to agree on one? That was going to take forever when they were all this great.

"No one is saying anything," Ian said nervously.

"Because they're all amazing, dude." Ella gave him a light punch on the arm. "All these years, and I never knew you were a pro graphic designer."

"It's nothing." He waved away the compliment.

Next, the fundraising subcommittee reported what they'd been up to. "I've been calling one local business every day, looking for potential sponsors," Ella said. "A lot of them have been surprisingly open to the idea."

"That's great!" Todd said. "Anything set up for sure yet?"

"Not yet. A bunch of them said they'd call me back, and if they don't, I plan to call back and harass them."

I liked the confident way she said that, and the determined set to her brow. She was definitely an interesting girl, and it seemed like we might get along better in person than Sam and I did.

We split into our subcommittees for the rest of the meeting. Ian and my other group members sifted through the potential poster options, trying to pare them down to one or two. I half-listened, but I was paying equal attention to Ella over in her group. She spoke often, and her voice carried through the room.

"I've been trying to contact the smaller, progressive companies that are more likely to want to associate themselves with LGBT stuff," she said. "Once I've practiced on those, I'll try my spiel on some of the bigger corporations."

"Judi, do you have an opinion?" Ian asked.

I turned my attention back to my own group. "You know, I honestly love all of these. Can't we use two or three?"

"Have multiple posters?" he asked with a frown.

"Why not?" I asked. "There's no reason that they all have to match. In fact, having two different designs could mean people will notice them twice as often."

"We could even target them to different areas," another man said. "Like, we could make one emphasizing the family-friendly events and put it up in school areas."

I tuned out, letting my eyes stray over to Ella again. She gesticulated as she spoke, and the fire in her eyes intrigued me. Despite her youthful features, her self-assured attitude ensured everyone would take her seriously.

For the most part, she'd been completely focused on her group's conversation. Now her gaze drifted over to me, and her eyes met mine with what appeared to be confusion. I gave her a tiny shrug and turned back toward my group. I'd been caught staring, and I didn't give a damn.

When the meeting ended, I walked outside with her and Ian again. Ian buzzed with excitement about his poster designs. "I'm going to make a family-friendly version, and I'm going to make the fonts bigger, and I'm going to put a QR code on all of them."

I nodded patiently, but he just kept talking. It was as if he'd finally found his life's purpose in making these poster designs.

Finally I interrupted. "Ian, maybe you should get home and start working on them."

He blinked. "Oh... I'm boring you."

"Not at all!" I said, trying not to grin.

"She's being polite," Ella said, looping an arm around him. "We're bored out of our minds, but it's okay. We love you anyway."

Ian shook his head. "And I love you both, even if you're jerks. I'll see you next time, right?"

"See you!" we both sang out, waving as we watched him head over to his car.

We turned to face each other, and I hugged my arms around myself. Even with my thick jacket, I got chilled by standing outside for more than a minute. The snow was ankle-deep where it hadn't been shoveled, and my boots would only keep the water out for so long.

"You're cold," Ella said.

"It's freezing out."

"We should get you inside somewhere. To your car, maybe."

Ah, she didn't want to come on too strong. "I was thinking about grabbing a tea to warm up," I said, trying to walk the fine line between casual and flirtatious. "If you'd like to join me."

Her eyes widened barely perceptively. "Sure, that sounds nice."

We decided to go to a coffee shop a few minutes away. It was close enough that we could've walked, but she insisted on driving to save me from the cold. I gave in, pleasantly surprised by her concern for my comfort.

When we'd both parked, we met inside. She ordered her drink and asked me what I wanted. I said I was still deciding, but she stood back and waited for me. Although I generally preferred to pay my way on a first date, even an unofficial one, my tea was only going to be a couple of dollars. And I already had a feeling this "date" was going to go a lot better than my last one had.

After letting her pay, we sat down and made small talk about the weather for a few minutes. The barista called our names, and after getting our drinks, we changed the subject to the Pride planning committee.

The topic was only mildly more exciting than

the weather. Of course I cared about Pride, but I'd just been thinking about it for an hour and a half. I wanted to hear about Ella – what she did for a living, how she spent her free time, what she thought about life and love and the universe.

Still, I was happy just to be here, watching her lips move as she spoke. She'd taken off her glasses and hung them in her collar when we sat down, and her eyes were even prettier than I'd imagined – a normal shade of brown, but they sparkled with personality.

"So…" She lifted her coffee mug, blew on the foaming milk, and set it back down again. "I assume things didn't work out with the girl you mentioned."

"Girl?" I frowned. "Oh, no. That was a guy. I'm bisexual."

I preferred to let people know that before the first date, when possible. Some lesbians took issue with my sexuality, and I liked to weed them out before things went anywhere. Still, five minutes into the first date wasn't too bad.

I'd never gotten around to telling Sam, now that I thought about it. Not that it mattered – things weren't going anywhere with him, either.

"Ah," Ella said. "I assume it didn't work out with him, then."

"I don't think so," I said. "He's a nice guy and all, just not for me. But I'm sure you don't want to hear all the dirty details."

She raised an eyebrow. "I'm fine with hearing the clean ones."

"Oh, I didn't mean it like that! It's a figure of speech."

Snorting, she picked up her mug again. "I know."

So she'd gotten me all flustered on purpose? This girl was more devious than I'd thought. I'd have to get her back for that somehow.

"Anyway, tell me about your love life." I gave her a cheeky smile.

"There's not much to tell," she said. "I don't meet women I'm interested in too often. Small-town life, and all. I'm not a fan of long-distance dating, either. Texting and phone calls just aren't the same as being there in person."

"You can say that again."

She looked up at me from beneath lowered lashes. "So… what kind of person do you go for?"

"I don't have a specific type, at least not physically," I said. "I'm a sapiosexual, really. I'm attracted to people's brains, not their genitals. When I look back at my exes, they all challenged me mentally. I like someone who can think on my level."

"Sounds a little pretentious, but okay."

I coughed on the sip of tea I'd just taken.

"You're really going to sit there and call me pretentious to my face?"

"If you say something pretentious, sure." She smirked.

"Wow." I shook my head, more amused than offended. Ella was quick to take familiarities with me despite barely knowing me, and I had to admit I liked that about her. "So what do you look for in a partner? And you better not have the tiniest hint of pretension in your answer."

"Someone who can put up with me," she said. "Who's breathing. Preferably with a pulse."

I had to laugh. "All right, I'll admit your answer was less pretentious than mine. There must be more to it than that, though."

"I was going to say 'who has breasts and a vagina,' but I'd be fine with dating a trans woman," she said. "I guess it's more like, 'who identifies as female.' I've been single my whole life. I'm not in a place to be picky."

"Seriously?" I shook my head. "Girls must be all over you. How have you not had a girlfriend yet?"

"Why would they be all over me? I'm cute, or something?" Her lips twitched as if she was suppressing a smile.

"You're adorable," I said. "I think I told you that already."

"Right." She rolled her eyes. "I'd rather you

described me as beautiful or hot or sexy, but I guess adorable is all right."

"I never said you couldn't be any of the others, too."

She ran a finger along the rim of her mug. "Anyway, putting up with me might be a harder task than you'd expect."

"I doubt that." I liked her more the more I got to know her. "What's so horrible about you?"

"Nice try," she said. "You'll have to find out for yourself."

I sipped my tea, keeping my eyes on Ella. I had a good feeling about her. I hadn't seen anything to suggest I wouldn't be able to "put up with her" for a good long while, or even indefinitely.

"What do you do, anyway?" I asked. "I don't think we've even covered that yet."

"I'm a librarian," she said with a smile. "I actually work at the branch we were just at."

"Oh, right! Ian mentioned that last time." I'd completely forgotten. "I'm a barista, by the way. I'm hoping to leave soon and find something in my field."

"What field is that?"

"Well... I took a very useful major. Gender studies. Employers have been banging down my door trying to give me a job." I shrugged self-deprecatingly. "I'm not exactly sure what I'll actually do with that degree. I might go back to school and get another certification. Maybe HR, PR… I don't know. I change my mind every day."

"That's funny," she said, staring at me more keenly than before. "Would you ever think about becoming a librarian?"

"Totally!" I'd just been telling Sam that was my dream job the other day. "I heard it's not that great and the job market sucks, though. Is that true?"

"Kind of." She was still looking at me funny. "I love the work, but it can be frustrating. And it's true that there aren't a lot of job openings. I was lucky to get my gig, and I'll be even luckier if I manage to advance anytime soon. There are so many junior librarians like me, and the senior ones are in no rush to retire."

"Maybe it's not the best plan for me, then." I picked up my tea with a sigh. "Every day, I wish I didn't have to work at all."

She squirmed in her chair as if my comment had made her uncomfortable. It'd been innocent enough, hadn't it? Maybe it was a weird thing to say to someone who actually liked her job.

"I better get going," she said. "I'm supposed to, um… look after my little sister."

Why did she look so shifty right now? Something was up. It was as if she'd lost interest in me out of the blue. But why would she have? I bit my lip, disappointed. I could handle being rejected – I just wished I knew why it was happening.

"All right," I said. "Um… did you want to exchange numbers? Just in case we want to talk before the next meeting." I was still interested, even if she might not be.

She hesitated for a moment. Goddamn, what had I done wrong? "Sure," she finally said. "I'll take yours."

She pulled her phone out and tapped it a few times. "So… it's J-U-L-I-E?"

"Oh! No," I said. "You must've misheard when Ian introduced us. It's Judi, actually. Judi with an I."

She stared at me again, looking like she was about to be sick. "Right," she mumbled. "Of course it is."

NINE – ELLA

Somehow I managed to make my way home despite my mind being in a frantic, unstoppable whirl. Julie, the gorgeous woman who'd piqued my interest two weeks ago… now appeared to be interested in me as well… which would've been perfect, except she was also Judi… the girl I'd been texting while pretending to be my brother!

When I'd realized it, I'd been so dazed that I lied and said I had to get home and look after Coco. In reality, that was one of the chores Sam had taken over in exchange for me helping him on his date with Judi.

As I came in the front door, I realized I actually could've told her I had plans with friends – because I did. I'd totally forgotten, swept up first by her magnetism and then by my own idiocy.

I waved to Sam as I passed the kitchen. He and Coco were at the table, working on her science fair project with glue guns and glittery beads.

"Hey!" he called. "It was my last day of work today! I didn't ask Judi out again in person, so could you text her and suggest dinner sometime?"

I paused in the doorway, feeling like I was going to throw up. "I'm on my way out," I said, sounding harsher than I'd intended.

"You didn't text her today, right, since we were both working? Or did you text her after we got off?"

I shook my head. I would've texted right after she got off work, but I'd been busy with the Pride meeting. The meeting she'd also been at. She'd even told me over text that she was doing volunteer work today. I hadn't connected the dots.

"Let me see your texts from yesterday," Sam pressed. Coco hummed to herself as she glued beads together, unaffected by our discussion.

"I told you, I'm going out!" I hurried up the stairs to my room and slammed the door behind me.

Once I was alone, I rubbed my hands over my face. What was I going to do? I couldn't even ask my friends for advice. The queer community was so small that word would probably get back to Judi. Or one of Sam's friends would overhear and relay the information to him.

Maybe I should tell him myself. I hadn't done anything wrong, although he was going to be *pissed* when he found out I'd clicked with Judi. It wasn't as if I'd *tried* to steal the girl he liked, but he was probably going to see it that way.

God! He was so into her, too. He was practically obsessed with her, and they didn't even have anything in common. She was a sapiosexual, and he was a dolt. A loveable dolt, but a dolt nonetheless.

I lay down and pressed my face into the pillow. Maybe he'd be more okay with this than I thought. He knew he wasn't as smart as her – right from the start, he'd said that was one reason he wanted me to speak for him. He'd known I could connect with her on her level better than he could.

But I had a feeling he didn't even know she was bi. That was going to make it even more of a kick in the teeth when he found out his sister had stolen his woman! Of course, that was assuming I'd be able to keep Judi's interest once she found out.

Unless… she didn't find out.

I sat up, my mind still racing. I needed to talk this through. Not with Sam, and definitely not with Judi… but with someone completely uninvolved.

That was how I ended up recounting the story over drinks with my friends an hour later. "I was reading this crazy thing on the Internet," I said, trying to sound as casual as I could. "This girl was talking to a girl online, pretending to be her guy friend, who liked her."

"Who liked who?" Deena asked. "The friend or the other girl?"

"The other girl." I inched my chair forward, making the creaky wooden table shake. "But it turned out the two girls met in real life, and they liked each other."

"How's that crazy?" Mindy asked. "Because they're lesbians? Lesbians exist, Ella."

I scoffed at her. Her joke would've been funny, seeing as we were all lesbians, but jokes were the last thing I needed right now. "Because the first girl feels like she betrayed her guy friend," I said. "She was supposed to make the other girl like him, not her."

"That's not her fault." Deena swayed in her chair. She was a lightweight, and it seemed like our first beer had hit her hard.

"No, it's not," I said. "But still, he's going to be mad. Wouldn't you be mad if something like that happened to you?"

"If I asked someone to text my crush on my behalf?" Mindy asked. "No, he was pretty much asking for this to happen."

Deena nodded. "Besides, this would never happen in real life. It sounds like something from a TV show."

"But even if the brother – I mean the friend – could accept it, the other girl would be mad. Wouldn't she?" I asked.

"This is fake!" Deena slurred. "Let's talk about something real. Like the *real* girl in Denver I started chatting with from OkCupid."

"She might not even be a real girl," Mindy

muttered. "There are so many fakes out there. Besides..." She turned back to me. "How would the other girl even know anything happened?"

"I don't know." The same question had been plaguing me since I'd realized who Judi was. "She might notice they type the same way, or something."

"Are you kidding?" Deena laughed. "She'd have to be, like, a CSI-level writing analyst."

"It could be something else, though," I said. Like if Judi found out Sam was my brother – then it'd be a thousand times easier for her to put two and two together. "I feel like these kinds of things always come out."

"Sure, on TV, where they happen." Deena drained her pint glass and waved to the waitress. "People keep secrets in real life. It's not like this girl would be lying about cheating, or something. It's not like she killed the other girl's puppy."

"Deena has a point," Mindy said. "It'd be like a white lie. It's not going to hurt the other girl."

I looked from Mindy to Deena, my stomach churning. What they were saying sounded so wrong. It went against my sense of honesty and transparency, the values I'd been raised with. And yet, they were both so sure of their way being right.

If I were to do as they said, I could have a shot at my dream girl. If I told her what'd happened, I could lose that chance forever.

The waitress appeared beside our table. "What can I get for you ladies?" she asked.

"A refill for everyone, and a shot of tequila for me," Deena said.

I thought about turning down the next beer – but fuck it. "A shot for me, too, actually."

*

The rest of the night was an alcoholic blur. No wonder I found myself lying in bed for hours the next morning, groaning in pain from my hangover. My head pulsed, and I could barely open my eyes enough to see the time on my phone. There was no way I was about to talk to anyone, or text them either.

I finally dragged myself out of bed around two. Wrapping myself in my warmest bathrobe, I inched my way downstairs. Although my stomach was still a bit queasy, I thought I could handle a glass of water and some toast.

Sam was in the kitchen, laughing as he watched a video on his tablet. I stopped short when I saw him. Last night, I'd decided not to tell him I'd met Judi in real life. In the clear light of day, with him right here in front of me, I wasn't sure if I could pull off that deception.

It'd feel wrong to keep something so huge from

my brother. We were open with each other. We always had been. Even in our teen years when we were supposed to be so hormonal that we hated everyone and everything, we'd been close.

Our home life had been somewhat unstable. Mom always had boyfriends coming and going. I had no memories of my dad, and only vague memories of Sam's. Mom had calmed down with her dating in recent years, but when we were younger, I sometimes felt like she cared more about her love life than about taking care of her kids.

Sam was only three years younger than me, so we'd been able to relate to each other for as long as I could remember. We'd relied on each other, for cooking and cleaning as well as for our emotional needs.

As different as we might've been, we were family. Nothing had ever gotten between us, and I liked to think nothing could. Not even a girl.

"What are you watching?" I asked, pouring myself some water and sitting down next to him.

He showed his tablet to me. "A reaction video about the game last night. See, they put Kyle Lennon's face on a baby's head because he acted like a baby when they lost."

Typical Sam. "Funny. Um… I think I'm going to give you your phone back. Then you can watch videos on there."

He paused the video. "I don't mind watching stuff on the tablet. It's actually better to watch stuff on the bigger screen."

He honestly thought I wanted to give it back for his benefit. "The thing is, well, I'm not so comfortable with texting Judi anymore."

"Why?" He looked at me sharply. "Did she start sexting me, or something?"

I choked on my water and spent a few seconds coughing before I could recover. With the way their date had gone, he honestly thought she'd want to sext him? The only reason she was even still talking to "him" was because of our amazing text conversation!

"No, I..." I'd been planning to tell him everything, and now I hesitated. I didn't need to tell him about the coffee date, did I? He didn't need to know I was interested in Judi at all. I could break it to him later. For now, I'd go with the gentlest option. "What happened is, I actually met Judi in real life. She's a friend of a friend. Now that I know her in person, I feel weird about tricking her like this."

What I'd said was true. She *was* a friend of Ian's. I knew Sam would assume I'd met her at the bar last night and not at the Pride planning committee, but that wasn't really relevant, was it?

"You met her?" He looked stunned, as if he hadn't expected Judi to have a life outside the coffee shop. "How do you know it was her?"

"Well, she said her name was Judi with an I."

"There are lots of girls with that spelling."

"She said she works at a coffee shop." *And the phone number she gave me is the same one I've been texting for two weeks,* I held back from adding.

"So you talked about Caffeine Hut?" Inexplicably, he looked excited now. "Did she say anything about me?"

"Oh… no." Not unless he counted the part about the date she'd gone on being disappointing. "She didn't say the name of the coffee shop, so I didn't tell her I knew who she was. I thought it might be weird if she knew we were siblings."

"What did you think of her? Isn't she amazing? And gorgeous?"

I cringed. "Yeah, she's pretty cool. We got along well."

"Hmm…" I could see the wheels turning in his head. He pushed the tablet aside and leaned his elbows on the table. "Maybe it's good that she doesn't know who you are. This way, you can ask her what she's thinking about me. Get some inside intel."

My stomach got even queasier. He wanted me to collect information for him, like some kind of a double agent? "I don't know if that's a good idea," I said slowly. "She's already pulling back from you, right? She said no to a second date. It seems like she's losing interest."

"But she hasn't given me a firm no, so I still have a shot."

I pursed my lips. "I don't know what I'd be able to find out in person that I couldn't have found out over text. We already know her interests and her hobbies, and a ton of other things you were supposed to bond with her over. Honestly, you didn't use that as much as you could've. You already had a giant leg up on every other guy pursuing her, and you still got nowhere." I was being a bit harsh on him, but he needed to hear this.

"That was different," he said. "She still thought she was talking to me. She'd be much more open with a new girl friend. If you were to drink some wine with her and have some girl talk, I'm sure she'd tell you all about her old relationships and the guys she's been into before. She'll tell you what other guys have done right or wrong, and then I'll be able to use that to make her mine."

To make her his? That actually sounded a little creepy! And he didn't even know her well enough to know he needed to worry about girls as well as guys. He obviously thought she was straight, so he didn't know much about her at all.

"Sam, you already had your chance," I said firmly. "If she's not into you, you need to accept that." And accept she was into me, when I eventually told him. "Besides, bonding over girl talk doesn't work quite as well when one girl is gay."

"Then tell her you're straight!"

I glared at him. Did he seriously want me to go into the closet so I could "bond" with Judi? This would go way beyond a simple favor. He'd owe me, like, years' worth of chores. "If you guys end up dating, she'll figure out I'm your sister, and she'll know I was helping you figure out how to win her over. She'll figure out I'm gay, too."

"We can cross that bridge when we come to it." He'd perked up completely, as if this new development had assured him he could still win Judi's heart.

"No, Sam. This has already gone too far. I'm not doing this for you."

He looked at the floor. "What do I have to do to get you to help me?"

"I'm not going to. Period." I pushed back my chair. "I'll give you back your phone, and I'll take over my chores again. This whole Judi thing is over. You're on your own."

"Wait. Ella…" The plea in his voice stopped me in my tracks. "I'll take my phone back. You don't have to text her anymore. But if you think she's cool anyway, and you might want to hang out… you could try to befriend her, couldn't you?"

"I'm not gathering information for you."

"No, no," he said. "Just be normal. You don't have to lie or pretend anything – although I'd rather not tell her we're siblings for as long as possible. Don't try to force any girl talk with her."

"What's in it for you, then?" I asked, skeptical.

"When she finds out I have a cool sister, it'll make me look better," he said, sounding sincere. "And if you do happen to find out anything that'd help my case, you can tell me."

"I don't know, Sam. This feels funny."

"You said she was cool, though." He looked at me pathetically. "You said you liked her."

Didn't he see that was the problem? I liked her *too much!*

But he was begging me, and he was going to keep going until I gave in. How was I supposed to explain why I wouldn't do it without giving everything away?

"Fine," I said, defeated. "I'll do it."

TEN – JUDI

Caffeine Hut felt different without Sam there. Even though he wouldn't have been scheduled over the weekend anyway, I could feel the lack of his presence. Or maybe it was just that Wren kept harassing me about him.

"What's going on with lover-boy?" she asked first thing in the morning. And then, "What's my old friend Sammy up to?" during a brief moment of quiet.

I told her over and over that nothing was happening between us. Still, she kept pressing the subject. I guessed I sounded unsure of myself when I told her I wasn't interested – which was the truth. As badly as that one date had gone, I was still intrigued by the Sam I'd been texting. I didn't want to let that go.

By noon, I hadn't heard from him. We usually said hi first thing in the morning. Maybe he was busy getting ready to start his new job – it had to be stressful for him. I tried not to care. If I wasn't going to be his girlfriend, I had no right to expect him to text me all the time. Once I rejected him properly, he most likely wouldn't want to text me at all.

I hadn't heard from Ella either, and that concerned me just as much. I still hadn't figured out why she'd gotten so turned off and left our coffee date so suddenly. I'd mentally reviewed everything I'd said a million times, and I still hadn't come up with anything that would've caused her reaction.

Midway through the afternoon, I found a moment to check my phone. To my surprise, I had a new message from each of them.

Sam: Hey cutie. What's up?

Ella: Hi, it's Ella from the other day. You know, the rude, awful one who told you you're pretentious. How are you doing?

Sam's message made me frown. He'd never called me "cutie" before, and if I was going to transition our potential relationship into a platonic friendship, I needed to nip that in the bud.

I dashed off a quick, curt response. *Hello. I'm working. How are you?*

Next, I reread Ella's message with a smile. She sounded mildly flirtatious, which made me more relieved than it really should've. Maybe she hadn't run away from me after all. Maybe she really just had to go home.

As if I could forget such a terrible person, I typed back. *I've been stewing in rage since we parted ways. What have you been doing since then? I need more things to hate you about.*

"Look at that smile!" Wren said. "Someone finally texted you."

"Huh? Oh…" I glanced down at my phone.

"Sam did text, but we're just going to be friends. I swear."

"That's not a friendly expression on your face," she said. "You look like the prince just rode in on a white horse and asked you to marry him."

"Well…" I pulled out a tray of cookies and rearranged them neatly, even though they didn't need it. "Someone else texted me, too."

"There's someone else?" she asked, her eyebrows shooting up. "Already? You don't waste time!"

"Nothing ever happened with Sam, okay? It's not like I'm moving on after a break-up."

"Sure." She sounded unconvinced. "So tell me about this new person."

"Not yet. Maybe if things go anywhere."

A customer came in, which meant she had to leave me alone. Almost half an hour passed before I was able to check my phone again. Again, I had two new messages.

Sam: Not bad. I was thinking we should get coffee sometime soon. As customers this time. He'd added a winky face.

I cringed. Hadn't I turned down his last attempt at asking me out? Clearly I hadn't been firm enough. I was surprised he'd even try to ask again. Normally we chatted and bantered all day, and now he was trying to meet up after one text? Maybe he was feeling bolder now that we were no longer coworkers.

I typed my reply carefully. *Sam, I'm sorry, but I've been really busy lately. I won't be able to meet up anytime soon.*

I sent it, then immediately kicked myself. Why hadn't I just told him flat-out that he wasn't my type? I wanted to stay friends, but not if he was going to be lusting after me and hoping it'd turn into more. I needed to be upfront and clear with him – but at the same time, I didn't want to hurt him.

Brushing away those thoughts, I flipped over to the other new text. *I had a quiet weekend,* Ella said. *Kicking puppies, punching babies – you know, the usual. What are you up to this week? Maybe we could grab a drink sometime.*

A flutter went through my heart. She was still into me, and her sense of humor matched mine completely. In fact, I liked her even more with every text she sent.

Cool down, Judi, I told myself. Hadn't I learned my lesson about getting excited about someone based on their texts? For all I knew, she could've been Googling what to say to me, too.

But no, I couldn't see her doing that. Her texts matched who she was in real life – they had the same voice, the same tone. She was clearly being genuine, whereas Sam... well, I had no idea what he was doing.

I think I can put up with you long enough to have a

beer, I texted back. *Maybe tomorrow night? I'm off work tomorrow and Tuesday.*

Her reply came back instantly. *Sounds like a plan. You can decide when and where.*

I chuckled to myself. *Wow, you're so difficult. So impossible to put up with.*

As I slid my phone into my apron, I noticed Wren's eyes on me. "You're going to have to tell me about this new person soon," she teased.

"Maybe." Heat rose to my cheeks. "We'll see."

*

The next night, I arrived on the dot of eight at the bar I'd chosen. It was one of the more openly LGBT-friendly places in town. While it wasn't a gay bar by any means, the sight of two girls kissing wouldn't be out of place. And I hoped I might reach that point with Ella by the end of the night.

I'd dressed in slim-fit jeans and winter boots, my short hair pulled into a tiny ponytail. With minimal make-up on, I looked much more boyish than I had for my date with Sam.

I only waited in the cold for a moment before Ella arrived, bundled up in her puffy olive-green jacket and a thick wool scarf with matching hat and gloves. Her glasses were dotted with melting snow, and she took them off to wipe them on her gloves before wrapping me in a hug.

"Look at you," I said. "Are you on your way to Siberia?"

"I get cold easily." She opened the door, letting me go inside first.

"You must have a hard time in the winter."

"The winter? Like right now isn't winter?"

"It's mid-December," I said. "The season's still getting started."

"Don't tell me that," she groaned.

The bar was nearly empty, so we took seats near the back so the draft from the door wouldn't bother her. It seemed like we were getting along fine again, and while I still didn't have a clue why she'd left so suddenly last time, the question was starting to bother me less as I became more confident of her interest in me.

We ordered drinks and nachos, then sat for a moment, just looking at each other. It would've been an awkward silence with someone else, but with her, I felt like she was doing it on purpose.

"Christmas," she finally said out of nowhere.

I raised an eyebrow. "What about it?"

Her eyes sparkled. "It's coming up! Are you a Christmas person? What are you going to do for it?"

"Oh, right." It was less than two weeks away.

"I'll spend some time with my family, but it's not a big deal for us. We don't do a big gift exchange or anything."

"So unenthusiastic!" She shook her head. "Christmas is the best time of the year, hands down."

"I would've thought summer would be your favorite."

"Nope. Christmas is worth every minute of cold." She tilted her head to the side thoughtfully. "At least, every minute leading up to it. After New Year's, it's a slow downslide into misery until the temperatures perk up again."

"You have strong feelings about this."

The waitress set our locally-brewed IPAs in front of each of us, and Ella took a gulp before responding. "Christmas is just amazing. My family does a Secret Santa, and we usually make something rather than buying a present, so we all get to be creative. Then we have a huge dinner, and all of us make our specialties – even my nine-year-old sister. I'm not a fantastic cook in general, but for Christmas and Christmas only, I make my famous cornbread and chorizo stuffing, and it's always a hit."

"Damn. Your family puts mine to shame."

There was nothing wrong with my family. We got along, although I had a few older relatives who were more traditional and didn't "agree" with every aspect of my "lifestyle," or what I'd studied in school. For my parents' sake, I could deal with their presence a few times a year.

A strange look darted across Ella's face – was that guilt? "What do you think about Santa Claus?" she asked, skilfully changing the subject. "Beloved symbol of childhood, or consumerist icon?"

"Neither," I said. "He's a tool for parents to trick their kids into behaving well when they're too young to know better."

"Go on."

I'd had this discussion with friends a few times over the years, and it seemed like my opinion was an unusual one. I cracked my knuckles, gearing up for the inevitable argument. My friends were always light-hearted when they objected to my thesis, but personally, I took it seriously.

"Kids believe whatever you tell them, right?" I asked. "They don't have a choice. They don't know anything about the world, so they count on the people around them to tell them the truth about what's going on. They trust them."

Ella blinked at me. "Right."

"We laugh at kids for believing in Santa. We think it's so cute that they fall for it. But why wouldn't they? He's right there in front of them, taking pictures with them at the mall. They see him with their own eyes! And how is it harder to believe an old man in a sleigh brings presents, than that drones from Amazon do? There's all kinds of magic that actually exists in the world we live in. Electricity, computers, the Internet. How would little kids ever have the critical thinking skills to figure out this one thing is a lie?"

"Well – " She tried to interject, but I wasn't done.

"So, think about it," I said. "Parents banded together to come up with this lie to trick vulnerable kids into believing Santa is real, and for what purpose? To make their own lives easier. They bribe the kids with the thought of presents, and if the kids are bad – a term which is defined by the parents – they'll get coal instead. It's straight-up bullying! And society completely accepts it. Encourages it, even." I let out my breath in a huff and took a swig of beer, waving at Ella to indicate it was her turn to speak.

"You're very passionate about this," she said dryly. "I do agree you have a point about the lying. I don't agree with lying in any context. On the other hand, parents aren't the ones to blame. They didn't create Santa. Corporations did. Coca-Cola came up with modern-day Santa in the 1930s."

I grinned. "That's a myth, actually. The Santa with the red suit and the white beard already existed before that, although I'll grant you that Coke popularized him."

As our debate went on, I reflected inwardly on how much fun I was having. Ella was an excellent conversational partner. First of all, she was adorable. I liked the way her eyes lit up when she talked about something she was interested in, and I definitely liked watching her delicate pink lips form her words. More importantly, she had a lot of opinions, and the knowledge to back them up.

Sam, on the other hand... I could just imagine how he would've stared dully at me during my rant. At the end, his contribution would've been something along the lines of, "Wow, you're so smart." Or he would've been frantically Googling under the table for something to say. God, I couldn't believe I'd been interested in him romantically for more than a millisecond.

The nachos arrived, and we eagerly dug in as our discussion continued. When the food was gone and our beers were drained, there was no question about what to do next. We ordered another, and then one more after that.

We touched on children's rights, the postmodern era, and the nature of reality, among other topics. Our conversation was flowing so well that I felt like she was an old friend. It was hard to believe this was only the third time we'd met, and the second time we'd properly spoken. I could already see that she was a kindred spirit – which was hard to find anywhere, and especially in this small town of ours. I could guess she was going to stay in my

life for a while, either as a friend or – I hoped –
as more than that.

"Oh my gosh, it's getting late," I said, looking at
my watch. It was past eleven, and I hadn't
thought about the time since we got here.

"Do you have to get home?" she asked
sympathetically.

"Like, do I have a curfew? No, I don't think my
roommate would give me one." I laughed. "I'm
not even tired. I just didn't realize how late it
was."

"Well, I'm having a good time talking to you,
and I don't need to be anywhere, either."

Hearing that made me smile. "There's no reason
to leave, then. You're not hungry or anything?"

"Oh, I'm always hungry."

We agreed to head to a pizza place a few blocks
away. They were open late, and after a few
drinks, the grease would be perfect to soak up
the alcohol.

We settled up our bill. Despite her protests, I
picked up the entire check. "You got my tea last
time."

"As if that evens things out!"

"It's all right. You can get my pizza." I was
daring enough to run a finger down her arm.
"And if that still doesn't square us up, you can
get my drinks next time."

As we headed back outside, she piled on her

clothes again – the coat, the hat, the scarf, the gloves. She looked like a bundle of rags – an adorable one.

"You're okay to walk over?" I asked, swaying slightly from the beer. "We could call an Uber, if you want."

"I think I can handle a five-minute walk," she laughed. "But actually, there's something I want to do first."

My heart stuttered. "What's that?"

She grabbed me by both shoulders, bringing me over to the side of the building, where no one could see us. "Something I've been wishing I could do since the moment I saw you."

I licked my lips, warmth building inside my core. If she was talking about kissing me, I'd been wishing she'd do that for quite a while now, too. I brushed a strand of hair back from her face, enjoying the brush of my fingers against her skin. The cold had made her cheeks go rosy, making her look cuter than ever. "Why don't you do it, then?"

Her lips turned upward, and she pulled me closer to her. I leaned closer, close enough to feel her breath on my lips. My heart raced as she stared into my eyes. Her face asked a question, and I only hoped she knew the answer was yes.

God, yes. She closed the distance between us, and my eyes fluttered shut as her lips landed softly on mine. Her arms linked around my neck, and mine laced around her back. She deepened the kiss, and I shivered. My desire for her had been growing all evening, and now that she was kissing me, it thrummed to new heights. With our winter clothes separating us, I couldn't feel her body heat, but the layers between us only made me crave her more.

This was really happening. I'd met a smart, sweet, *sexy* woman, and she liked me too. I'd been waiting for this to happen for what felt like a million years, and now Ella had appeared out of nowhere, like an angel out of heaven. I wished I could stay in this moment forever, my first kiss with my future girlfriend. Ella… Ella… *Ella.*

"So," I breathed when she pulled away. "Pizza? Or…?"

She took my hand, wrapping my bare fingers in her gloved ones. "I think I might need to head home."

I stared at her. "You mean, you want me to go home with you?" I would've thought my place would be a better option – but I had a sneaking suspicion that she wasn't talking about me coming with her at all.

"I mean alone."

"You're not up for getting food?" I asked.

Slowly, she shook her head.

Why was she pulling this hot-and-cold act again? She'd been the one to kiss me, and now she was going to run away? What happened to at least getting pizza?

"Um… okay," I said. "Text me, then?"

She looked at the ground. "Of course, Judi."

Eleven – Ella

The day after my date with Judi, the library was quiet. Hardly anyone bothered me. This peacefulness would've been welcome on a normal day, but today it gave me the perfect environment to stew in my guilt.

I wished a drunk would come in and start yelling at the other patrons, or that one of the little kids in the picture book section would throw up all over the floor. Anything to make me stop thinking about how perfect Judi was, and how awful I'd been to her.

I moved through the stacks, mindlessly searching for books that had been requested for interlibrary loans. The date last night was one of the best I'd ever been on. Probably *the* best, when I put everything together – her gorgeous looks, her sparkling conversation, and that heart-melting kiss.

I should've been on cloud nine today. I'd found the girl of my dreams right here in my own town, and she was into me. She'd even suggested going home together! I could've been with her for real, if my conscience hadn't gotten in the way. I couldn't go through with it when I knew I'd been lying to her.

But what was I supposed to do? I couldn't tell her I'd pretended to be Sam. But at some point, wouldn't she figure it out for herself?

I never should've agreed to "help" Sam with this. What had I been thinking? A week or two off chores, in exchange for a lifetime of regret? I was such a fool.

Seeing the Dewey decimal code I'd been looking for, I grabbed the book and tossed it onto my cart, noticing the title for the first time. *Ethics and Interpersonal Relationships.* I pursed my lips. Maybe I should've given that one a read before I got myself into this mess.

When five o'clock came, I headed home. I was supposed to cook tonight, but I'd start later. I had a little time to work on my Christmas present for Mom, who I'd gotten for our Secret Santa. I was cross-stitching her a quote that she liked: "You never realize how weird you are until you have a kid who acts just like you," with a woman and girl as stick figures.

I'd been working on it for months, and it was coming along at a snail's pace. I was starting to stress a little about it. There were only eight days left to get it done.

I turned on a Luscious Karma album, cringing as I remembered talking about them with Judi. I was such a piece of shit! I picked up the needle and jabbed it through the fabric, then immediately cursed because I'd jabbed it straight into my finger.

I stuck my finger into my mouth, biting down to stop it from bleeding. I wasn't sure if that was how it worked, but I didn't mind – more than anything, I just wanted to make myself hurt.

The front door creaked open, and I shoved the cross-stitch under a couch cushion in case it was Mom. The reality was even worse. Sam breezed into the living room, brushing snow off his shoulders and all over the floor.

My stomach churned as I looked at him. I'd betrayed him last night, too. He'd die if he knew I'd kissed his crush. They weren't dating, he didn't have any claim on her – *technically* I hadn't done anything wrong… but he wouldn't see it that way, and I knew it.

"Oh my God, it's only a little snow," he said, seeing my expression. "It'll melt."

I pulled my cross-stitch back out and pretended to be completely absorbed in it. "It's fine. Whatever."

"Stop being like that. I'll clean it! You're better at guilt-tripping than Mom." He left, giving me enough time to hate myself a little more before he returned with some paper towels.

He scrubbed at the wet spots on the floor while I stared blankly at my craftwork. Maybe he'd clean up and leave, maybe he wouldn't ask anything about Judi. I could hope, anyway.

"How'd it go with Judi last night?" he asked, trying and failing to sound like the question was off-the-cuff. "What'd you two do?"

Fuck. I'd thought about this moment, tried to

plan for it, but now that it was here, I was thrown off-balance nonetheless. "We had a few drinks," I said, probably sounding just as phony to his ears. "Had a nice talk."

"Yeah? See, I knew you two would get along!"

I nodded, my stomach sick. *That's the problem, don't you see? We get along too well!*

"What did you talk about?" he pressed.

"All kinds of things," I said. "Life, the universe, Santa Claus…"

He took the cross-stitch out of my hands and set it aside, sitting on the floor in front of me. "Did you talk about *me?* That's what I'm asking."

"No," I said. At least I could be honest about this part. "We didn't."

"You were out so late," he said, heaving a sigh. "I thought you definitely would've gotten some intel out of her if you spent that much time with her."

"What, were you waiting up for me?" I glared at him. "I told you, this wasn't some kind of secret spy mission to get you laid. I went because I thought Judi could be a cool friend."

"It's not about getting laid. You know that." He grabbed my knees, looking like the little boy I remembered he'd been not so long ago. "I like her *so much*, and I don't even get to see her at work anymore! If you don't figure out a way for me to get through to her, I might never see her again."

"Sam, you told me she turned down your last suggestion for a date." *And she accepted mine the same day,* I didn't add. "When are you going to take no for an answer?"

"I already did. I know she rejected me... but she was interested at first. That means I could still get her back if I can impress her properly."

"I don't think that's how it works." I pulled my legs out of his reach, tucking them under me on the couch. "She isn't going to give me some magic passcode you can say and win her heart. If you're not right for each other, you're not right for each other! There are plenty of other girls out there – ones that'll like you just as much as you like them."

He sighed. "I know."

For once, he didn't follow that up with a reason that he should still keep trying. Maybe I was getting through to him, and he'd leave her alone. Then I could figure out how to tell him I'd succeeded where he'd failed.

"How's the new job going, anyway?" I asked. "I didn't get a chance to see you last night." He hadn't gotten home until after I left for my date with Judi.

"It's okay," he said. "My new boss took me out for lunch yesterday. We got spicy wings."

I stared at him. "I mean the actual work, not the lunch you ate."

"It seems okay." He shrugged. "I don't really know how to do half the things I'm supposed to be doing, but I'll pick it up as I go along."

I frowned. "What kind of stuff?"

"Spreadsheets, software, invoices…" He shrugged. "Google was invented for a reason, Ella."

"If you're sure." I picked up my cross-stitch again. I was dubious about his ability to pick all of that up on the fly, but from what I'd heard, confidence went a long way in an office setting. If he could bullshit his way through it, he might be okay. It wasn't time for an intervention – yet.

He got up, then paused in the doorway. "Ella?"

"Yeah, I'm going to start cooking soon."

"No, no." He looked self-conscious. "I was just wondering… do you really think I lost my chance with Judi?"

He seemed so pathetic, there was no way I could tell him the truth. "You and Judi are very different," I said carefully. "I think you might be more compatible with somebody else."

"So she said something bad about me." Panic took over his face.

"I told you, we didn't talk about you." I rubbed my temples. "Look, you have her number. Why don't you talk to her yourself?"

"You know what?" he said. "Maybe I will."

TWELVE – JUDI

I handed a bottle of mustard to Chelle. "Check this, please. Does it pass approval?"

She was pickier about her food than I was, and although most roommates might not have shared their food, we found it easier to buy things like condiments and spreads together. She always ended up picking pricey organic stuff I wouldn't have paid for on my own, but it always ended up tasting better than the regular stuff, too.

"This has preservatives in it," she said, wrinkling her nose. "All mustard should have is vinegar, mustard seed, and a couple of spices."

"All right, I'll let you find something to satisfy your gourmet palate. Somebody's texting me."

I dug my phone out of my purse, already hoping the message might be from Ella. I hadn't heard from her since Monday night, which was far too long. I didn't want to come on too strong, so I hadn't texted her either, but I was pretty sure she knew I wanted to hear from her.

She was probably too busy with Christmas preparations to text. At least, that was what I was hoping. She'd cut our date short so suddenly, and then I hadn't heard from her for two days... It didn't bode well for our potential relationship.

I knew she liked me, but something was making her conflicted about seeing me, and I couldn't guess what it was. Could there be someone else in the picture? An old crush that she hadn't gotten over? Maybe she was having health problems, or there were issues with her family. I didn't know, and not knowing was the hardest part.

After mentally sifting through the events a thousand times, my best guess was that I'd been too forward, turning her off by talking about going home together. But that would've been a natural progression from what we'd been doing – why would it have been so shocking?

My heart dropped when I saw the text was from Sam. I'd kind of been hoping he wouldn't contact me again. He didn't text me to chat anymore – his last message had been about going for coffee, which I'd said no to. Couldn't he take a hint?

Hey, his message read. *My new job is boring and it sucks that you're not here. How are you doing?*

Worse now that you texted me, I wanted to type. It was funny to think I'd once valued his friendship and wanted to stay in touch. His recent texts had been so blah, I wondered how I'd ever found him interesting.

I slipped my phone back into my purse instead of replying. My face must've betrayed my disgust, because Chelle laughed at me. "I'm guessing that wasn't the cutie from the coffee shop."

"It was, actually. Ugh… I'm so over him."

"Then why have you been glowing all the time?" She dropped a bottle of organic Dijon into our shopping cart. "I was sure you were starting something up with him."

"Ah, no… although there is someone else."

"Oh, really?"

"But I don't know where things stand with her right now, so…"

"What's the issue?" Chelle spun around to examine the rows of ketchup. "She doesn't like you?"

"She seems to, but then she runs away. It's already happened twice."

"Is she seeing someone else? Or struggling with her sexuality?"

"No and no, as far as I can tell." I sighed. "I can't figure out what the problem is."

"Have you, y'know, asked her about it?"

I stared at her in horror. "I can't do that."

She took a ketchup bottle off the shelf and examined the nutrition facts. "Why not?"

She sounded so casual, as if what she was saying wasn't absolutely blowing my mind. I *could* just ask Ella what was up, couldn't I? I could communicate with her and have a conversation about why she'd left so suddenly.

"I can try," I said slowly.

"It should work better than standing around and wondering about it." She smirked at me.

I huffed at her. "Just for that, we're getting Heinz." I dropped a bottle in the cart and dragged it out of her reach.

*

When we got home, we unpacked the groceries together. I'd given in and let her get a eight-dollar banana ketchup. She deserved it for the life advice she'd given me. I was going to call Ella and see if she'd tell me what was up.

First, though, I'd reply to Sam. I couldn't avoid his message forever. *I'm good,* I wrote. *Sorry to hear your new job isn't so great. Hope it gets better soon. Talk to you later!*

That was about as harsh as I could get when it came to him. He was like a puppy – I didn't want to hurt him.

Sitting on my bed, I dialed Ella's number. After four rings, she picked up. "Hello? Judi?"

"Hey!" I said, my heart pounding at the sound of her confused voice. "What's up? How are you doing?"

"Not… bad." She paused. "How about you?"

"I was just thinking about you," I said, toying with the edge of my blanket. "Actually, to be honest, I've been thinking about you for the past two days."

"Ah."

Ah? That didn't exactly give me a lot of confidence. I was hoping for something more along the lines of her thinking about me, too.

Still, I pressed on. "Look, I wanted to talk to you about the other night. I had a great time, and it seemed like you did too, but then you cut things short out of the blue, and I can't stop asking myself if I did something wrong or said something to offend you. If I was too forward by mentioning going home with you, I sincerely apologize. I don't want you to think I'm just looking for a fling. I really like you, Ella." I ran out of words and took a deep breath, trying to calm my jangling nerves.

It took her a moment to speak. "I'm sorry I confused you like that. I didn't realize how abruptly I left."

"Okay." I waited for her to go on.

"The thing is, Judi, you're amazing. You're seriously so, so amazing."

I could sense a "but" was coming, and she didn't disappoint.

"But… I'm not sure if it's a good idea to keep seeing each other."

I swallowed hard. I'd known this might be coming, but it still hurt to hear. "I don't get it," I said in a small voice. "We had such a nice time, and then you kissed me. Did I… did I have bad breath?"

"No! Not at all."

I folded my legs under me, my heart aching. "I can accept if you're not into me like that. I just wish I could understand."

She hesitated again. "I *am* into you. I…"

"I want to see you again," I blurted out. If she was going to reject me, she could reject me, but at least she'd be doing it in person. "Can I see you again? Tomorrow night. We'll go for pizza."

"I'd love to, Judi, but…" She paused, and I held my breath, praying she was talking herself into saying yes to me. "You know what? Sure. Let's get some damn pizza. It's not going to hurt anybody."

"Great!" I grinned, pumping a fist in the air. "I'll see you tomorrow, then? I'll text you and we can figure out the time."

"Sounds good."

As we hung up, my elation faded. Sure, I was going to get to see Ella again, and that was great – even if I'd had to beg her for the date.

But I still didn't know what her problem with me was. And that meant we still hadn't solved it.

THIRTEEN – ELLA

I wasn't lying to Judi. All of the dishonesty was in the past, and at this point I was being completely honest. That was what I kept telling myself as I drove toward the pizza place where I was meeting her.

If she asked whether I'd pretended to be someone else over text, I'd tell her the truth. It wasn't a secret – it just hadn't come up yet! I didn't have to tell her every little thing I'd done in the past. She probably wouldn't even have cared.

All right, maybe that was pushing it.

But still, she liked me. A lot, she said. For some inexplicable reason, she was determined to go out with me again, and I wasn't strong enough to say no to her.

If things moved forward between us, she'd find out Sam was my brother soon enough. I'd tell her the whole truth one day. It wouldn't even be a big deal. We'd probably laugh about it!

I wasn't lying to her anymore. I just wasn't ready to tell her yet.

I pulled up in front of the pizza place and got out of the car. She was already waiting outside, her bright red hair flecked with snow. She waved brightly when she saw me, and once I was close enough, she hugged me hard enough to knock the wind out of me.

"Someone's excited," I laughed.

"Sorry." She gave me a shy smile.

Now I remembered I'd made her think I wasn't interested in her, and I felt terrible. I would never have thought she'd even care if she saw me again, but apparently she did.

"Let's go in before you freeze," she said. "They have an amazing Hawaiian pizza here."

"Are you one of those heathens who thinks pineapple belongs on pizza?" I asked, holding the door for her.

"Pineapple was made for pizza," she said, taking my arm as she led me to the counter. "Try it and find out."

"I've had pineapple on pizza before, Judi."

The cashier shook her head. "You haven't had our Hawaiian. It has back bacon, extra cheese, and Sriracha sauce."

I scanned the menu. "Sounds good, aside from the pineapple."

Judi tightened her fingers around my bicep. Even with my coat between us, her touch made me weak. I couldn't help but remember the other day, when her lips had brushed so sweetly against mine. A shot of desire went through me.

"Try it," she said. "How bad could it be?"

Although it still sounded horrible, I was quickly realizing I'd do anything for this girl. "Okay," I said. "Sign me up."

She squeezed my arm. "You'll be a convert in no time."

"We'll see about that." I took her hand and led her to a booth by the wall.

When we sat down, she laid her hand over mine. "Thanks for coming tonight, Ella."

I cringed. "Don't say it like I'm doing you a favor. I want to be here, I promise. I just... it's complicated."

"You're not seeing someone else, are you?"

"No!" I was horrified at the thought. "I'd never cheat on anyone. And honestly, if there was anyone else in my life, I'd probably have already broken up with them for you. You're pretty damn special."

She went pink. "What's going on with you, then? Are you sick? Dying? Planning to move to the other side of the planet?"

"Good guesses, but no." Extracting my hand from hers, I stared down at the table. "I can't tell you right now. I'll tell you eventually, though."

"That's not suspicious at all." She laughed.

"Everything's on the up and up, I swear. It's hard to explain."

She tipped my chin upward with her finger, forcing me to look into her eyes. "It's nothing that would hurt me?" she asked.

"No." *Kind of. Maybe.*

"Then let's not worry about it anymore," she said softly. "I don't know what the problem is, but I trust you. If you say it's not a big deal, then I'm going to treat it like it's irrelevant."

My heart pounded. *Was* it irrelevant? The only way to know for sure would be to tell her and see what she thought. I licked my lips, suffused with guilt.

She must've taken that as a hint, because she leaned across the table. "I'd really like to kiss you right now."

I shouldn't kiss her when I didn't know how she'd feel about the Sam thing. I couldn't! And yet my lips parted of their own accord.

Her breath touched my skin, and I felt her eyelashes flutter against my cheek as my own eyes slowly closed. Her lips brushed against mine, tentatively at first, and then with more passion. My heart beat faster as I leaned in, running a hand along her shoulder, then lacing my fingers through her hair. She smelled like strawberries and she tasted like chocolate, and...

A cough came from beside us. "Your pizza, ladies."

We broke apart, and I tried and failed to catch my breath. I cleared space on the table for the pizza pan, avoiding the waitress's eyes.

"Enjoy." Sounding amused, she left.

"That was so embarrassing," I whispered to Judi. "Are you ready to die? I'm ready to die."

"Taste this pizza," she said, picking up a knife. "Then you'll have something to live for."

"I doubt it. I should probably just die right now so I won't have to suffer through it."

She cut the pizza and placed a slice on each of our plates. At least it looked good aside from the pineapple. The cheese was thick and gooey without looking greasy, and the back bacon sizzled as if to prove it'd just come out of the oven.

She lifted her slice and took a bite. "Mmm!" she said. "This... is... orgasmic."

A twinge went through my body, and I wondered if I might get to hear her say those words again tonight.

She opened her eyes to look at me. "Sorry. I mean... try it!"

Cautiously, I picked up my slice. There was no pineapple on the tip, so I bit down and let the flavors explode through my mouth. The bread, the cheese, the bacon – this actually was pretty close to orgasmic.

"Try the pineapple," she said, her eyes bright and mischievous.

"I'm not going to like it, just to warn you."

"All I'm asking you to do is keep an open

mind."

My mind was already open, thank you very much. Why would this Hawaiian be any different from any other that'd been foisted on me over the years? Still, I'd eat it for her sake. I took another bite, allowing a pineapple cube to slip past my teeth. I braced myself as I chewed – and then I paused in surprise.

"I see that look on your face," she crowed. "You love it, don't you?"

The pineapple was sweet. Tangy, even. Paired with the salty bacon and creamy cheese, it created a flavor combination in my mouth – a new and exciting combination.

I chewed a few more times, holding up a finger. This pizza was *excellent,* but I wasn't going to admit it.

I swallowed. "Okay, it's not bad."

Judi's eyebrows shot up. "Not bad? Not bad? You think this is *not bad?* Do you think the Mona Lisa isn't bad? Would you say Beethoven's Ninth is just all right?"

I took another bite, a bigger one this time. "You're very passionate about your pizza."

"You didn't answer my questions." She glared daggers at me, then narrowed her eyes. "I see how you're digging into that. You think it's amazing. You can't even deny it."

I licked my lips, darting my tongue out to catch

a stray bead of tomato sauce. "All right, fine. This pizza is fucking mind-blowing."

She sat back in her seat, looking vindicated. "The pineapple, too?"

I bit into a cube of it, and the tanginess tantalized my taste buds. If I lied, she'd see right through me. "Yeah, yeah," I muttered. "The pineapple, too."

*

By the time the meal was over, we were getting along like old friends. I'd admitted that occasionally, in rare instances, pineapple could be good on pizza, and for her part, she seemed to be relaxing around me, too. She acted like she'd stopped thinking about my weird behavior earlier, and I hoped that was really the case. The longer we could go without talking about it, the less I had to feel guilty about keeping the truth from her.

"What do you want to do now?" I asked, wiping my mouth with a napkin.

"Well…" Her eyes glowed. "I'd love to listen to some of the music we were talking about, if you're up for it. I have some awesome speakers at my place."

At her place. I knew exactly what she was actually saying, and my nerves tingled at the thought of it. I stroked a finger along her hand and watched goosebumps prick up along her arm. Would I be a horrible person if I did this without telling her about the Sam thing?

"I'm being too forward again," she said suddenly. "I'm sorry. I don't want to pressure you at all. You don't have to come home with me just because it's our third date. We can take things at your pace."

I boggled at her. Did she honestly think I didn't want to be with her? I would've given my left arm for this! "It's not that," I said. "I'm ready – more than ready."

"Then let's go." She leaned across the table to peck me on the cheek, and the imprint of her lips tingled long after she drew away.

"Okay," I whispered.

We took our separate cars to her place, and I vibrated with anticipation. I still wasn't quite sure if this was real. It felt too good to be true.

When I pulled up at her house and came inside, and she grabbed me and kissed me, sliding her hands under my coat and around my waist, I knew I couldn't have dreamed anything this good.

"So," she said, her face flushed as she took off her coat. "Let's listen to that music, then? In my room?"

My pulse racing, I nodded. "Sounds like a plan."

Her room was as warm and inviting as she was. The walls were painted a soft yellow, and a large window opened onto the street. The speakers she'd mentioned were set in each corner of the room, large black towers that promised high-quality surround sound.

She laughed as she saw me eyeing them. "I take my music seriously."

"I can tell," I said.

She connected her phone to the Bluetooth. "Give me a second. I'll play you something amazing. I just discovered this band recently, and I'm absolutely addicted."

Not Luscious Karma. Not Luscious Karma.

"They're from the Denver area, actually," she said, still focused on her phone. "They mix folk music and indie pop, and it ends up being the most incredible sound."

The opening twangs of the song I'd first recommended to her started up, and I forced a smile onto my face. "You mean Luscious Karma! Oh my God, I can't believe you've heard of them."

"You know Luscious Karma?"

"They're one of my favorite bands."

Her jaw dropped. "I've been telling everyone I know about them for weeks, and no one has heard of them. This is such a crazy coincidence!"

My lips trembled with the effort of keeping the

smile pasted onto my face, and I turned away so she wouldn't see it turn into a grimace. "I know a few people who are into them, actually."

Vaguely, I wondered if I was passing up the right moment to tell her I was "Sam." But I couldn't bring up that conversation now, when I was in her room for the first time. There'd be a better time later, when we weren't both thinking about the same thing.

"What else do you like to listen to?" I asked. "Maybe you could introduce me to some of your old favorites."

"Sure, yeah. That's a shame, though. I was looking forward to blowing your mind again." She blushed. "With their music, I mean."

A flame of desire lit up in my core. "I guess you'll have to find some other way."

"That wasn't what I meant!" A giggle escaped her. "Although it's still true."

I came toward her and kissed her again. Kissing her had been utterly unimaginable not so long ago, and yet now it was quickly becoming familiar, even comfortable. I was getting used to the fireworks that went off behind my eyelids every time my lips met hers; in fact, I was starting to wonder how I'd ever lived without them.

"We should get on the bed," I murmured.

The darkness in her eyes betrayed her lust. "You first," she said.

I backed up to the bed, pulling her along with me as I tugged off her top. I traced a finger along her collarbone and along the curve of her breast, down to her bra cup. The softness of her skin amazed me, and I couldn't seem to stop touching her.

"You have an incredible body," I breathed.

"It's just a body." She gave a shy laugh. "It gets my soul from point A to point B."

She unbuttoned my shirt, taking her time until my nipples pebbled in anticipation. When she took off my bra and ran a palm over my breasts, a surge of desire went through me, so strong that my knees went weak.

We tumbled onto the bed together, touching and kissing and nibbling everything we could. I was finally here with her. I'd been wanting this girl for weeks, but it felt like I'd been waiting for her all my life.

I brought my lips to her neck and sucked in a bit of skin, wanting to leave my mark on her.

She giggled. "That tickles."

I caressed her silky hair, her narrow shoulders. "This is about to tickle a lot more."

I lowered my head and flicked my tongue across one nipple, then the other. Her breath hitched, and she let out a groan. She lay back, holding her hips up as if asking me to strip off her pants. Once I did, I brought a hand between her legs, searching for her heat.

"Ah," she gasped, her walls clamping down on my exploring finger. "Fuck – Ella – you feel so good."

"I haven't even gotten started."

Staying inside her, I brought myself down to lie between her legs. This, right here – this was where I'd wanted to be since the first moment I saw her. I kissed her inner thigh, nibbled my way closer to her center. I had her wriggling and bucking before I even grazed my tongue over her clit.

"Oh God," she breathed, her hands lacing around the back of my head. "Oh, *fuck*."

I loved the sound of her moans. I loved that I was the one making her feel that good. Her hips juddered under me as I swirled my tongue around and around. Her wetness dripped down my finger, and her musk rose to my nose. Her pleasure would be my only focus until I made her come – and then until she came a few more times, if she could handle it.

As if on cue, her legs began to shake. "Ella," she groaned, grabbing even tighter onto my head. "Don't – fucking – stop!"

I kept going, not stopping as her body seized up, or as she let out an ear-splitting cry. I only slowed down once her ragged breathing had returned to normal, and even then, I didn't stop until she physically pushed me away.

"Okay," she panted. "I can't take any more."

I pulled myself up to her side, a little breathless myself. "That's a shame," I said. "Let's rest for five minutes and see how you feel then."

"I can take a break for five minutes, but I'm not going to be resting." She slipped a hand underneath my panties, finding the spot that had been aching for her since we got here. "Oh wow, you're so wet."

"For you."

I let her take off my pants the same way I'd taken off hers, then parted my legs as she slid between them. She caressed my hip, looking up at me with open, genuine excitement. "I'm so happy we're here. I'm so happy I met you."

"Me, too."

I lay back, shivering as her tongue made contact with my spot. But her words echoed in my mind, and the guilt that had faded away while I was focused on her returned with a vengeance. What would she think if she knew I'd "met" her before she met me? What would she say if she were to find out?

She squeezed my thigh. "You seem tense. Are you nervous, Ella? Try to relax."

I bit my lip. I should've been in the throes of ecstasy right now, and instead, I could only think and fret and worry. "Sorry," I said. "I'm just a little in my head. Keep doing what you were doing, it feels amazing."

But even as she went back to pleasuring me, I

knew I wouldn't be able to relax until I told her the truth.

FOURTEEN – JUDI

Christmas passed without much fuss. I spent a few hours at my aunt's place, making small talk with my extended family and trying to ignore the jabs they made at my education and the job it had gotten me. At least the food was good. My aunt made amazing turkey, and a few of my cousins were absolute pros at baking.

I'd texted Ella often over the past week. We hadn't found time to see each other again since our pizza date, but considering how it'd gone, I was fairly confident that was just because of the holiday season. As soon as Christmas was over, we'd make time for another date.

It turned out that the Pride planning meeting on the twenty-seventh wasn't canceled, as I'd expected it would be. Todd had emailed and said he'd considered canceling, but since the holiday season could be tough for a lot of LGBT folks, he'd decided to run it as usual despite expecting a smaller turn-out.

Ella and I decided we'd attend, then go out afterwards. I told her she was welcome to stay over if she wanted, which she hadn't given me a definite answer to. Since she lived with her family, she'd have to tell them she was seeing someone if she spent the night somewhere. I guessed she might want to be more serious about me before doing that – but selfishly, I still wanted her to.

The twenty-seventh finally came, and I met Ella at the library desk. She'd been working today, and I was grateful for the chance to see her in her natural habitat. Even after she took off her badge, she still looked obviously like a librarian with her glasses, her cardigan, and her hair in a bun. I licked my lips as I looked at her. I was starting to develop a librarian fetish.

"Hey," she said, wrapping me in a tight hug. "Merry Christmas."

"Merry Christmas!" I held her close, wishing I could kiss her with all the passion that I felt. If we hadn't been at her work, in front of her coworkers, I would've done it. "You had a good time with your family?"

"An amazing time."

She'd already updated me via text about the cross-stitch she'd done for her Secret Santa, which she'd barely finished on time, and her cornbread and chorizo stuffing, which she said she'd outdone herself on this year. I had to admit, I envied her closeness with her family. Even so, her enthusiasm for Christmas was contagious, and she'd inspired me to do something in the holiday spirit myself.

"This is for you." I handed her a small parcel.

"You didn't." She smacked me playfully on the arm. "It's our fourth date, Judi. You honestly shouldn't have."

I shrugged. "It's not much, but I think you'll like it."

"Should I open it now or later?" Her eyes were glowing, which told me I'd done the right thing.

"Whenever you'd like." I couldn't hold back from pecking her on the cheek. "It's seriously nothing, though. If you try to build up the anticipation, you might be disappointed."

"But look how cute the wrapping is." She toyed with the purple ribbon that I'd carefully coiled into a bow. "I don't want to wreck it."

"Okay, you're making me nervous. Open it now, before you get your hopes up too high."

Perching on the library desk, she carefully tore the package open. I watched her face, my own anticipation rising. Even though the gift hadn't been expensive, I'd put some thought into it, and I couldn't wait to see her reaction.

"A T-shirt!" she said, shaking out the fabric. "It's... Oh." A strange expression passed over her face – I saw shock there, for sure, and them something else. Disgust? Pain?

"It's official Luscious Karma merchandise," I said quickly, holding it up for her as if she hadn't seen the logo on the front already. "You said they're one of your favorite bands, so I got it off their website. I wasn't sure of the size, but..."

It did seem a bit large for her. Was that why she looked upset? Had getting a medium made her feel like I thought she was bigger than she was?

"This is… wow." She looked at me and her lips smiled, even if her eyes didn't. "So nice of you. Thank you."

"You hate it, don't you?" I didn't need to be a mind reader to figure that one out. "Are you not that into them? Or do you not like band T-shirts?"

"No, it's perfect. I love it." She gave me a chaste kiss on the cheek.

We headed over to the boardroom for the meeting, although I was still wondering where I'd gone wrong. Ella was so hard to read sometimes. Was this mood shift related to the ones she'd had before – the "complicated issue" she'd refused to talk about?

I sat down beside Ian and the other members of the marketing subcommittee. Almost everyone was here, despite the date. The meeting was about to start, so I took notes on my phone as Todd talked about our progress and what we still had left to do.

My subcommittee was going to have to start spreading the word about the festival soon. Ian and a couple of the others agreed to put up the fliers around town, and I told the group I'd set up a Facebook event and post some tweets about it.

When the meeting was over, I turned back toward Ella. "Ready to go?" I asked, placing my hand on her knee.

Ian peered over my shoulder. "Wait, what's this?"

Oops. I hadn't even thought to ask Ella if she was okay with people knowing about us. These were early days, and I wasn't sure if she'd told anyone at all about our first few dates. Now the cat was out of the bag.

"What?" Ella said to him, grinning. "Are you really surprised? You introduced two super-cute queer women to each other, and you're seriously going to be shocked that we'd end up dating?"

Heat rose to my cheeks. I knew she thought I was cute, but *super*-cute? And it was a thrill to hear her say out loud that we were dating.

"Okay," Ian said. "Maybe I should've seen this coming."

"You think?" I teased, exchanging a self-conscious smile with Ella.

"How long has this been going on?" Ian asked. "Are you a couple?"

"Just since the last meeting," I said. "So, two weeks. We're still feeling things out."

"Well, thanks a lot for keeping me in the loop." Ian tried to glare at me, but ended up beaming at us instead. "Seriously, though, I'm so happy for you two. I can see why you'd get along."

My heart warmed. I hadn't wanted or needed his approval, but it still felt nice to have it.

"I was going to ask if either of you wanted to hit the mall to see the sales," Ian said. "Guess you've got other plans, huh?"

"Slightly." Ella looped an arm around me.

"I'll just have to do my shopping by myself. Hmph!" He picked up his clipboard of meeting notes. "Have fun, you two. And if you happen to come across any super-cute single guys, throw them my way. It'd only be fair."

"We'll keep an eye out." I squeezed Ella's hand, and we walked out of the library.

I wondered if I did know any guys who'd be good for Ian. He was such a sweetheart, and he'd been single as long as I'd known him. I wondered what kind of guy he went for. I didn't know too many men in the first place, except for... hmm... Sam. I laughed to myself. As far as I knew, he was straight, so that might not work out.

"What's so funny?" Ella asked, pushing open the front door.

A gust of cold wind hit us. "I was thinking about who I could set Ian up with," I said. "I had the most ridiculous idea to pawn this one guy off on him. The last guy I was interested in before I met you."

"Sam?" She sounded shocked.

I was equally surprised. "I told you his name?"

"Um... you must've mentioned it. Why would he and Ian be good together?"

"They wouldn't. Sam's straight, and they have nothing in common. That's why it was funny."

"Ah, now I get it." She visibly relaxed.

"You know, sometimes I don't have the slightest idea what goes on in your head," I mused out loud.

"Sometimes I don't, either."

"So mysterious. I like it." Tightening my scarf around my neck, I paused in front of my car. "So I'll meet you at my place. You remember the route?"

"I GPS-ed it, and I'll be following you." She gave me a lingering kiss that set my body alight with possibilities. "You're going to make me dinner when we get there?"

"Eventually." I pressed my body against hers, and all the layers of winter gear between us couldn't keep me from getting excited by the feel of her curves. "There are a few other things I want to do first."

FIFTEEN – ELLA

Two weeks into January, and I'd been seeing Judi for a month. We hadn't put any labels on our relationship, but since neither of us was dating anyone else, it was hard to not think of her as my girlfriend.

I still hadn't found the right moment to tell her I'd once pretended to be Sam. As time went by, it seemed like less and less of a concern. Why would she even care, now that we'd spent so much time together? She knew me, the real me – the one that screamed like a little girl while tobogganing down a hill, the one that cowered in her arms during the scary part of a movie. I wasn't keeping anything from her in the present moment.

I couldn't say the same about Sam. He still mentioned Judi from time to time, getting a hangdog expression whenever her name came up. He was aware that we'd "hung out" a few times, but he still had no idea it was anything more than that.

It felt strange and unnatural to keep something like this from him. I couldn't even tell the rest of my family out of fear it'd get back to him. I was normally so open with them, and keeping secrets from them wasn't something I wanted or enjoyed.

One day after work, a soft impact hit me in my mid-back as I walked up the driveway. "Hey!" I yelled, spinning around to find Sam with his hands dusted with snow. "I thought we called off the snowball war this year!"

"We did because you were helping me out," he said. "But that's been over for so long, and your back looked so snowless. It was just begging for some of this."

"Oh, really?" Luckily I had gloves on. I reached down and scooped up some snow, quickly shaping it and jetting it back at him. "Then you won't mind this!"

"No, I don't." He ducked out of the way just in time. "All's fair in love and war."

An interesting choice of proverbs. Did he really believe that? "I'll get you with this one," I said.

"No, you won't!" He launched another snowball at me, and it flew past me – and right into the front door, which my mother had just opened.

"Kids, I just made hot chocolate," she called, then pointed down at the floor. "Although one or the other of you is going to clean this mess up before either of you is getting any."

We headed inside, kicking snow off our boots and shedding our coats. Hot chocolate sounded amazing right now. Once the snow was cleaned up, we went into the kitchen and served ourselves from the pot on the stove.

"I guess the new job is going well," I said,

dropping marshmallows into my mug. "At least, you seem to be in a good mood."

"It's going all right," he said. "I'm catching on to the spreadsheet stuff. Sometimes I miss my old job, though."

I looked at him sharply. "The coffee?"

"More like the coworkers." Holding his mug in both hands, he sighed. "Really just Judi."

Fuck. How was he still this into her? Why was he even still thinking about her? They had nothing in common. Nothing! They'd been on one date. It was like he was obsessed!

"I'm not in love with her or anything," he quickly reassured me. "She's just kind of my 'one that got away.'"

"You don't text her anymore, do you?"

"No." He hung his head. "I probably made a mistake when I asked you to text her. She got used to talking to you, and then she expected so much when you gave my phone back to me. I couldn't have that kind of conversation."

"So you haven't talked to her in a while?"

"No. She blew me off pretty hard, and I figured I'd wait and see if she ever reached out to me. She never did."

That was a bit of a relief. I hadn't even realized a tiny part of me had been worried she might still have some interest in him. "Sorry to hear that. It would've been nice if you could stay friends."

"How is she?" he asked, looking at me sadly. "Is she seeing anyone? Does she ever mention me?"

"Sam, if you're thinking about reaching out to her again, I would just say… don't." My tone was sympathetic, yet firm. "She already gave you her answer."

"I know! I'm not going to. I just wanted to know. It's weird for me, knowing you two still talk."

My heart stuttered. This might've been a good moment to tell him the full truth.

"But whatever," he said. "I'm not trying to keep you from having friends. It's nice that you two get along."

Tell him, Ella, just tell him. "Right."

"Lord knows you could use a new friend," he said. "You always hang out with me, Mom, and Coco. You need to get a life!"

"At least I know how to do my job," I said. Our teasing back-and-forth felt comfortable, whereas telling him the truth would've been very much the opposite. "Anyway, haven't you met any new girls yet? There are so many fish in the sea."

"Not like Judi," he said sadly.

I looked at his despondent expression, and I knew I wouldn't be able to tell him anytime soon.

*

Judi and I went on more dates, and afterwards we often went back to her place to explore each other some more. Her body was addictive, and I was thoroughly hooked. I could stay in bed with her all day – and sometimes I did.

She always said I was welcome to spend the night if I wanted, and I kept making excuses for why I couldn't. I'd once told her I didn't sleep well outside of my own bed, and another time I'd made some vague comments about needing to be home for Coco. Every time I lied to her, I felt guiltier and guiltier. But at this point, it would've been too hard to explain the truth.

This whole thing had started off so innocently. How had I ended up trapped in a web of lies?

I should've been on top of the world. I finally had a girl in my life, and she was as beautiful and unique and amazing as I could've ever hoped. She was crazy about me, and she seemed to be here to stay – but instead of being happy, I was constantly drowning in worries that the whole thing would come crashing down on me.

Any day now, something was going to have to give. Once one little thing came out of place, the rest would tumble down along with it.

And that day came sooner than I expected.

Judi and I were strolling around the winter market downtown one Sunday evening, her looking at handmade goods and me hugging myself and trying to stop shivering. "Ooh, this would look adorable on you," she said, holding up a knitted scarf. "The color really sets off your eyes."

She looped it around my neck, giving me a peck on the nose and then turning me to face the mirror. "It looks perfect," she said, hugging me from behind. "I'm going to get it for you."

"Judi?" A familiar voice came from behind us, and I saw Sam's reflection approaching us in the mirror. "*Ella?*"

Shit. Shit, shit, shit. "Hey!" I said, unspooling the scarf from around my neck and handing it back to the confused vendor. "How are you? I didn't know you were going to be here!"

"You two are *dating?*" Sam asked, looking back and forth between me and Judi, his eyes filled with questions. "What? How? When? Why?"

"You two know each other?" Judi asked, taking a step away from me and frowning.

"We're – " Sam started.

Shit! Why hadn't I come up with a game plan for this situation? What was I supposed to do now? What could I possibly say?

The jig was up when it came to Sam, and I'd have to explain everything and apologize later – but Judi still didn't know we were siblings, or that I'd tried to help him to date her. If I could keep her from finding out a little longer, I could delay the inevitable.

Although it *was* inevitable that she'd find out, so what was the point of putting it off? I didn't know if there was a point.

And yet the words were already spilling out of my mouth. "Yes, we know each other," I said brightly while also giving Sam a hard stare. "What a small world! You two know each other, too?"

"Sam was my coworker at Caffeine Hut," Judi said. "He's moved on to greener pastures. How's that new job of yours?"

"Good," Sam said, still staring at us with wide eyes. "I just… You're gay?"

"No, but I'm not straight, either." Judi laughed.

"So, we're going to continue with our date." I took her arm, my heart pounding. "See you around, Sam."

Judi and I took a few steps before she spoke again. "Well, that was awkward."

"That's the guy who was interested in you?" I asked, as if I didn't already know the answer.

"Yup." She picked up a bottle of locally-grown jam and pretended to look at it. "It's funny, men are always so shocked to find out I like women for real. They always think me being bi is some sexy performance for them, not that I'd actually date a girl. Although I don't think I ever came out to him in the first place, so it's no wonder he was a bit surprised."

"Right." I wished she had come out to him – that would've made that scene a whole lot easier.

"How do you know him, anyway?" she asked.

We came out of the same vagina. "Just… around," I said tightly.

"Neighbors? Friend of a friend?"

"Something like that."

I was only digging my hole deeper. She *would* find out, and when she did, these lies would only make her reaction worse. I could stop the madness and tell her now. I could say "Actually, he's my brother," and we could laugh about it.

Even if I didn't tell her the truth about the texting right now, at least I wouldn't be adding on another lie. A lie of omission was still a lie, and I was betraying her more with every moment that I kept my relationship to Sam a secret.

Judi shrugged. "Ooh, apple butter? I love that stuff!" She took off for a stand a few feet away, leaving me speechless in her wake.

The moment had passed, and I still hadn't told her.

SIXTEEN – JUDI

When I got home from the winter market, I settled on the living room couch. Chelle and Sabrina were already there, cuddling under a blanket, and I said hi to them without the familiar feeling of mild envy coming over me. They were still as adorable and perfect together as they'd always been, but now I didn't need to be jealous. I was pretty much part of an adorable couple myself.

I pulled out my phone, still thinking about the run-in with Sam. Ella's reaction to seeing him had been odd, and he'd reacted strangely as well. His behavior was understandable since he hadn't known I liked women… but hers?

Why would she be so weird about seeing him? I would've thought they'd dated or something, if I hadn't known she was completely and openly gay. She'd even mentioned that she'd never needed to experiment with guys.

Her answer about how they knew each other had been vague, like so many other things she said. She was clearly hiding something, and she'd never gotten around to explaining the "complicated" thing that she'd said she would tell me about later.

If she wasn't going to be upfront with me, maybe someone else would.

I opened a new text and addressed it to Sam. Our last chat had been more than a month ago. I'd liked him so much at the time – at least the text version of him. It was strange to think about how easily he'd slipped out of my life. I'd started texting Ella so much once we started dating. It was almost like she'd taken his place.

Hey! I wrote to him. *Funny seeing you today. It's been forever.*

I hesitated, wondering if I should make some small talk before getting to my real question. With my luck, he'd take it as a sign of renewed interest, so I decided against it.

How exactly do you know Ella? I added.

I set my phone on the table, making sure the sound was on so I wouldn't miss his reply.

"Waiting for word from the lovely Ella?" Chelle asked, flipping through channels. "I thought you just saw her. Why didn't she come over?"

"She had some other stuff to do." Although she hadn't mentioned not coming over until after we'd run into Sam, so maybe that had something to do with it. I didn't know.

"She seems so sweet," Sabrina said. "We should really double-date sometime."

"Yeah, I can ask her about it." And she'd probably give me some vague non-answer to that, too.

Dammit, this was bothering me more than it

should. Why did it matter if she hadn't given me a clear answer? Wherever she knew Sam from, it wouldn't be a problem for me. Unless they'd met in a club for punching puppies, I couldn't think of a reason why it would even affect me.

And yet she'd been so shady about it!

I grabbed my phone, hoping Sam had replied. He hadn't, of course – I would've heard the beep if he had.

"Why are you so eager to hear from her?" Chelle asked. "Are you two sexting?"

"No, we're not sexting!" I said. "Let me live! Jeez!"

"Well, we know you have a healthy sex life," Sabrina said with a smirk. "You kept us up late the other night."

"We did?" I asked, horrified. "I'm sorry! I had no idea."

"The walls are thin," Chelle said, leaning her head on Sabrina's shoulder. "We could hear every word."

"And every moan," Sabrina added. "You two are definitely enthusiastic."

"Oh my God!" I grabbed my phone and scurried into my room.

If this relationship went on, I was going to have to look into soundproofing.

*

By the morning, I'd nearly forgotten about the message I'd sent to Sam. Since it was my day off, I slept in until almost noon. I lay in bed reading a pop-psychology book for another hour before even looking at my phone.

Sam had texted back late last night. *Just from around,* he'd written. *I'm not even sure where we met.*

I frowned. That was a vague non-answer, too, which made me suspicious. But why would he lie? What would he have to hide? Maybe they really were in a puppy-punching club!

I slowly got dressed, taking my time with my hair and make-up. I didn't have any plans for today, other than working on the online marketing for the Pride stuff. I could do that from here, or go to a coffee shop – although I rankled at the thought of heading in to Caffeine Hut on my day off.

The other option was to go to the library. Hmm… I could see Ella. Surprise her.

And if she was up to anything funny, dropping in on her without notice might tell me something.

Not that I was trying to spy on her. Not at all.

I headed to the library around two, knowing she'd be working. Once I got inside, I looked around for a minute. Then I brought the book I'd found to the check-out desk.

"I'd like to check this out, please." I handed her the book.

Her eyes widened when she saw me. "Judi, what are you doing here? And what..." She looked down at the book and choked on a laugh. "What do you need this for?"

The book was *The Joy of Lesbian Sex*. "I thought I could use some tips," I said. "Don't you think?"

She came out from behind the desk and gave me a quick hug, When I let go, she hung on, looking into my eyes. To my surprise, she leaned in again and kissed me on the lips. As usual, the feeling made me tingle, and more so because she'd kissed me in the middle of her workplace.

"Is it okay that you did that?" I whispered. "You don't mind your coworkers knowing about me?"

"Why would I mind them knowing I'm dating a cute girl?"

"I guess I thought you'd want to wait until we were official," I said slowly. "You haven't even brought me around your family, or anything."

A veil dropped over her eyes. "That's different."

"How?"

She shook her head as if shaking the question off. "It's good to see you! I was honestly just thinking it sucked I wouldn't get to see you today. You should come in here more often."

"Yeah, I'm going to grab a seat and work on the Pride stuff." I nodded at the book. "I don't really need that, by the way… unless you think I really do need tips."

"We could all use some tips," she laughed. "But maybe I'll get you your own copy. We don't know where that one's been."

"True. You never know who's been touching it with… sticky fingers." I had a sudden urge to wash my hands.

She slid the book into the return bin. "We have hand sanitizer, if you want it."

I allowed a smile to spread across my face. This girl could pretty much read my mind. And she was gorgeous, and witty, and she'd been ready and willing to kiss me in front of all of her coworkers. If I'd come here hoping to catch her at something – and I had no idea what – I'd failed miserably. This visit had only made me fall for her a little harder than I already had.

Clearly she hadn't told me all of her secrets yet. But that was okay. If she wasn't ready to open up about certain parts of her life yet, I'd wait for her. She was worth it.

And I trusted her.

Seventeen – Ella

Sam paced around the kitchen, his panic so thick I could actually feel it. "How long is this going to go on, Ella? How long am I supposed to pretend I'm not your brother?"

"I don't know."

"I thought you had a plan when you asked me to tell her I knew you from 'around.' How is this supposed to work?"

"I don't know!"

As much as his questions were upsetting me, at least this was better than his initial reaction when I got home the other day.

"How could you do this to me, Ella?" he demanded.

"I'm sorry," I said. "It just happened."

"It didn't just happen! Things don't 'just happen.' You made it happen. Admit it! You decided you wanted her for yourself, and you asked her out."

"That's not true! I already met Judi and asked her out before I'd even known she was the girl I was texting."

He stared at me. "You asked her out when you met her through your friends?"

"That's not exactly what happened," I said. "We actually met at the Pride committee. I thought her name was Julie at first! Once I figured it out, I didn't

know how to tell you."

Once he understood the mistaken identity, he was a little more sympathetic. Still, he was far from happy that I'd "stolen his girl," and he only reluctantly agreed to pretend we weren't related.

"You told me you're serious about her," he said, rubbing the back of his neck. "So how's it going to work when she meets the family? 'Hey, this is my mom, my sister, and that guy I know from *around*'?"

"I didn't think about it!" I said, bile rising in my throat. "I should've told her you were my brother, but then I thought she'd figure out that I used to text her. I just freaked out and said I knew you from around. It was a spur-of-the-moment thing. I didn't think it through!"

"And then instead of having me clear things up, you asked me to add onto your lie," he said incredulously. "Now we've both basically told her we're not related, so how do you plan to keep her from ever finding out?"

"For the last time, I don't know!" I shook my head. "This all could've been avoided if you'd just told me you were going to the winter fair."

"Oh, I'm sorry. I didn't know I had to give you an exact report of my comings and goings in case I ended up running into you on a date with my crush that you stole from me!"

I hung my head. I was supposed to be the smart

one of the two of us. It was a sad day when Sam made more sense than me.

"Okay, I fucked up," I said. "What do you think we should do next, then? I really like her, and she seems to feel the same. She even came to my work today."

"Rub salt in the wound, why don't you?" Glaring at me, Sam leaned against the counter. "I think you should tell her the truth."

"I can't do that!" Maybe I could've done it at the start, but not now. I was fully invested in this relationship. Although I wouldn't have said it out loud, I was falling in love with Judi. She was everything I wanted and more, and there was no way I'd do anything that might ruin that.

"But how can you not?" Sam asked. "This isn't easy for me to say, you know. Telling her I needed your help is going to make me seem like some kind of pathetic loser."

"You said it, not me."

"Shut up." He crossed his arms. "The truth is going to come out, one way or another. The only choice you have is *how* she's going to find out. Do you want her to hear it from you, or do you want her to find some baby pictures of us on Facebook?"

"Oh God, I have to take those down."

"Ella, she's going to find out!"

I stood up and paced like he'd just been doing.

"Okay, maybe I can admit that you're my brother. I'll tell her we were joking around about where we knew each other from because... I'm ashamed of you."

"Try again."

"You're ashamed of me."

He rolled his eyes. "Come on."

"All right, we were joking around for fun." I got to the door, swiveled, and paced back toward the kitchen island. "The part about the texting never needs to come out. Ever."

"Don't you think she's too smart to fall for this?" Sam bit his lip. "I feel like you should just be honest with her."

"You're right. She knows me. She's going to guess I was the one texting her as soon as she finds out we're related." I stopped in front of the wall and stared blankly at its smooth coat of paint. "I don't know what to do, Sam. What do I do?" I'd really hit a new low if I was asking him for advice.

"I already told you," he said.

"No! There has to be something else."

He bit his lip. "What about this? Tell her I asked you for help talking to her. That I told her I like the bands and shows you like, because I guessed your tastes would be closer to hers. You can even say I asked you for help coming up with all those witty one-liners. You were just doing it for fun, and you had no idea you'd ever end up meeting her."

"Hmm… that could actually work."

"It's going to work," he said. "I'm letting you throw me under the bus here, Ella. I'm going to seem like a huge loser, but I'll let you do it because I'm a romantic at heart, and the two of you seem really good together."

"That's sweet of you." I still wasn't sure, though.

"You two are going to be able to make fun of me for this every single time you bring her to a family occasion until the day one or both of you dies."

I stared at him, not sure if I should laugh or punch him. I liked the idea of us making fun of him… and of bringing Judi to family occasions… and of being with her until death did us part. I decided to give Sam a smile.

"Maybe you're right," I said. "A half-truth is better than a lie, right?"

"I'm right sometimes." With a smirk, he grabbed me to stop me from pacing and pulled me into a hug.

I extricated myself, not quite ready to forgive him yet. "You know this whole mess is still because of you, right?"

"I guess. Kind of." He hung his head sheepishly. "Maybe just a little bit."

*

Now that I had a game plan, I was eager to put it into play. I wasn't going to tell Judi the "truth" via text. I wanted to do it in person, so I waited until our next date the following night.

We'd planned to watch a new nature documentary at her place and cuddle up. As soon as she opened the door, I took her hands. "Let's sit down for a minute before we watch the movie," I said. "There's something I want to talk to you about."

A look of worry crossed her face. "This sounds serious."

"It's nothing bad. I'm not breaking up with you or anything." Since she looked relieved, I laughed. "I wouldn't break this off for all the money in the world."

"Then what do you want to talk about?" she asked as we went up the stairs.

"I feel like I should explain some of the things that have been going on. I haven't been completely honest about everything." Realizing this sounded bad, I rephrased. "None of it is a big deal – I hope you won't think it is, anyway – but I've been hiding something from you, and I need to stop doing that."

"Okay." She sat down on her bed, gesturing at me to sit next to her.

I clasped both of her hands. "It's about my family. You know how I told you I have two siblings, right? A sister and a brother."

"Right." She looked completely lost.

"My sister is nine," I said. "Her name is Coco, and she's the sweetest little thing you've ever met – even if she can drive me insane sometimes, too."

"Okay." She blinked a few times, and I wondered if she was connecting the dots – if Sam had mentioned Coco to her, too.

"My brother is twenty-one," I said slowly. "His name is Sam."

She inhaled sharply. "Wait."

I nodded. "He's a bit of a dumbass, and he can be incredibly thick, but he also has a good heart, and he's one of my best friends in the entire world."

"You're saying your brother is the Sam that we ran into." She gripped my hands, as if that'd help her understand. "Sam from Caffeine Hut."

"That's correct."

"But you look different," she said, squinting at me. "Your personalities are completely different. You have different last names!"

"We have different dads," I said. "Same with Coco. We all grew up together, and we still live together. And when Sam didn't know how to talk to the cute girl at his work, he thought I might have a better sense of what girls like."

"He went to you for advice about me?" she asked, wide-eyed.

"Yeah." Silently, I thanked Sam for coming up with the half-truth that was so much less risky than the full version. "He could see we were kind of similar, so he asked me what kind of stuff smart girls are into, and then he pretended he was into it himself."

"The serial killer documentary," she breathed. "I knew he'd never watch that himself. I *knew* it!"

"And Luscious Karma," I said with a self-conscious laugh. "You thought it was such a big coincidence that I'd heard of them."

"Then you were weirded out when I gave you their shirt," she said. I could see her mentally connecting the dots. "Why, though? Why was it such a big deal? You could've just told me you'd helped Sam talk to me."

"He was embarrassed, for one thing." *Thanks for the permission to throw you under the bus,* I mentally told Sam. "He likes to pretend to be this cool guy, and he's really more like a kid underneath."

"Oh, I noticed!"

"But also, it wasn't just the movies and music," I said. "Sometimes he'd even show me your texts and ask me what to write back."

"Oh my God." She snickered. "That's…

something." She gave me a light shove on the shoulder. "I can't believe you actually helped him!"

She was taking this much better than I'd even hoped. If she could laugh about this, we were golden. "I didn't know it was you," I said. "I had no idea we'd already met, or that I'd end up clicking with you."

"Sam was right about one thing, anyway. We do get along." She brought her lips to mine, and for a long moment, I let myself drown in her soft kiss. "How's he feel about this, anyway? Now that he knows, is he freaking out?"

"He did at first, but I think he'll be all right," I said. "He seems to understand that you and me are more compatible than you and him would've been."

"I'll say."

I linked my fingers through hers. "It's definitely been odd to think about my little brother lusting after you, but it seems like everything's worked out for the best in the end."

"You must've been so scared to tell him we were dating," she said. "Is that why you were so hesitant to tell me who he was?"

Sure, let's go with that. "Yeah," I said. "I really thought I might hurt him. He was super, super into you."

"I hope it won't be weird when I meet your family."

I liked the way she took for a given that she'd meet my family. "It'll be okay." I put my arms around her. "I'm so happy I told you."

"Me, too. This explains so much." She shook her head. "I kept thinking Sam was so different over text. He was like a whole different person."

I stiffened. Did she suspect anything? Did it even matter at this point? She'd accepted the first half of my confession so readily – would she be equally calm if I told her the whole truth?

I wasn't going to find out. Telling her this much had been terrifying enough. I wasn't going to risk her outrage. I'd gotten away with what I'd done, and I was never going to lie or mislead her again.

"Ready to watch that movie now?" I asked.

"The nature documentary? Sounds good." She poked me. "Do you really want to watch it, or did you ask someone else for their thoughts on what you should pretend to like?"

"I really want to watch it," I said, kissing her neck. "Although to be fair, I'd watch anything at all if it meant being next to you."

EIGHTEEN – JUDI

The couple of weeks leading up to mid-February were a little stressful for me. I'd never dated someone who was so into the holidays before. Since Ella was all about Christmas, I assumed she'd be even more into Valentine's Day.

I hadn't asked her straight-out what she thought about it, not wanting to ruin the surprise. I figured she'd say it was no big deal when really she'd be secretly hoping to be wined, dined, and romanced into the night.

She had a tendency to downplay her own needs and wants, often putting other people before herself. She wouldn't want to make me go out of my way for V-Day, but she didn't know I'd be happy to if it made her happy. For this particular occasion, I just wasn't going to give her a choice. I was going to take her out and treat her like a princess, and if she thought it was too much, she was going to have to deal with it.

One bad thing about living in a small town was that there was only one fancy restaurant to go to. I called them a week in advance, and they were already completely booked up for the night of the fourteenth. I cursed to myself.

But… fuck it. I was thinking too small, anyway. If I wanted to give Ella a nice Valentine's, I should make a whole romantic weekend out of it. We'd drive to Denver, four hours away, and I'd get a hotel room. It'd be a bit of a road trip, so we could get out of town for a night and revisit our old stomping grounds from our college days. Sometime during the weekend, I'd ask her to be my official girlfriend.

And the walls at the hotel would be thicker than the ones at my house, so we could be as loud as we liked.

I found a nice restaurant in Denver and made reservations there. I assumed Ella would be up for staying the night. She'd admitted the only reason she'd refused to before was because she didn't want to tell Sam about us, and now that he knew, she'd started to stay over every weekend.

It was actually cute how nervous she'd been to tell me about him. I wasn't sure why she thought I'd mind. Sure, it might be a bit awkward to have a former date in my partner's family, but I figured that'd be more awkward for him than for me.

Valentine's fell on a Friday, and I called her the night before to hint at what we'd be doing. "Pack a nice dress in your overnight bag," I told her. "You might have some use for it."

"Wait, is this a Valentine's thing?" she asked.

"You'll find out."

I picked her up from the library after work, and

she frowned as we passed the highway exit to my place. "Where are you taking me?"

I pointed to the back seat, which was overflowing with bags of chips and bottles of pop. "Dig into some snacks. We're going to have a long drive."

"What? Where are we going? We're leaving town? What did you plan, Judi? Tell me!"

I just smiled and kept my eyes on the road.

"If I guess, will you tell me if I'm right?"

"Sure."

"Are we going skiing?"

"No."

"Are we flying somewhere?"

"No."

"Are we going to Denver?"

I stayed quiet, but I couldn't stop myself from smirking.

"You're taking me to Denver?" she screeched. "For Valentine's?"

"Is that a problem?" A rush of fear came over me. I was practically kidnapping her. I hadn't even checked if she was okay with going so far from home.

"I wasn't expecting this," she said.

"In a good way?"

She reached into the back seat and tore open a bag of Doritos. "I think so. We'll see."

*

We arrived in Denver just in time for our nine o'clock reservation. I'd had my pedal to the metal for the last hour of our drive, and even though Ella had offered to take over, I hadn't wanted to stop for that long.

"Next time, we'll allow some wiggle room," I panted as I finally parked.

She took my hand. "I like how you're already planning the next time."

The maître d' seated us, and we flipped through the menu. The prices were even higher than I remembered them being on the website. Since I was paying the gas and the hotel room, this weekend would end up costing a decent chunk of change – but Ella was worth it.

"I'll get dinner," she whispered.

"That's okay," I said. "It's Valentine's. I'm treating you." I scanned through the menu a second time. God, even the appetizers started at twenty dollars.

"Don't be silly," she said. "Let me do this." She took the menu out of my hands and flipped to the entrees before placing it back in front of me. "I *know* you want more than an appetizer."

"Well, if you insist."

The meal was delicious, although the servings were tiny. "We might have to pick up some pizza after this," I whispered when the time came for us to pay the bill.

She put her credit card down. "With pineapple?" she asked, her eyes sparkling.

"Always!"

We left hand in hand, and I reluctantly let her get in the driver's seat of the car. "Sorry," I said. "I really wanted to make this the best Valentine's Day of your life, but I can't drive a minute longer. I'm exhausted."

"It's already the best Valentine's of my life," she said. "I've never done anything for it before."

"Because you never had a proper girlfriend?" I buckled my seat belt and put my hand on her knee, wondering if this was the moment to make her *my* proper girlfriend.

"Yeah," she said. "That's part of it."

"We should change that."

She'd just put the key in the ignition, and now she froze and looked at me. "How do you mean?"

"We should get you a proper girlfriend."

A spark of hope lit in her eyes. "Yeah? Like who?"

"Oh, I don't know." I couldn't resist the urge to

tease her a little. "There's a cute girl who works at the coffee shop with me. Maybe I could get you her number. I could even advise you on what to say to her."

She put her hand over mine, and the heat of her skin warmed me. "I don't know," she murmured. "I'm pretty interested in somebody else. In fact… I'm falling pretty hard for her."

I turned my palm up, sighing at how good it felt when my fingers interlaced with hers. "Who is she?" I asked. "Do I know her?"

"I'm serious, Judi." Her eyes met mine, and she used her free hand to stroke my face. "I'm falling for you."

"I feel the same way." I pecked her forehead. "So this means you'll be my girlfriend?"

"Of course." She turned her head upward so that my lips fell against hers. "I love you."

*

Once we checked into the hotel, we tore at each other's clothes with more urgency than ever. Now that we were an official couple, now that we'd said the L word, I needed her like never before.

I barely saw our surroundings, too focused on her body. I loved getting her out of her work clothes. When she took off her glasses and shook out her bun, she went from a sexy librarian to a sexy *woman.*

Once I had her down to her bra and panties, I palmed her ass. "I brought a few toys in our overnight bag," I murmured. "In case you wanted anything."

"Right now, all I want is you."

She claimed my lips in another kiss, her tongue darting into my mouth and stroking my own. Heat rose in my core, and I knew no toys were necessary. With the two of us alone, I'd still be very, *very* satisfied.

We made our way to the bed, where we fumbled at each other as if fighting for dominance. After a moment, we lay side by side, her hand between my legs, mine between hers. Every flick of her fingers sent shudders through my body, and judging by the sound of her moans, mine were doing the same to her.

I turned onto my side so I could look her in the eyes as we pleasured each other. I'd never felt so close to anyone else. What we were doing was so intimate, so vulnerable. I brought my lips to hers once more, and the soft way they yielded to me drove me even wilder.

"I love you," I murmured into her mouth, feeling my excitement rise higher and higher. Now that we'd said those words, I wanted to keep saying them all the time. "Fuck... Ella... I *love* you!"

The climax tore through me, leaving me dizzy and breathless. Ella's lips found my collarbone, her free hand teasing a nipple as she drew the orgasm out, making it go on and on until I couldn't take it anymore.

"It's your turn," I said, gesturing at her to straddle my face.

"Mmm… have I mentioned I love you lately?" she asked, climbing on.

This was better than the best Valentine's Day I could've imagined.

Nineteen – Ella

Judi and I spent a perfect weekend together in Denver. I took her to the gay bar where I'd been a regular for two years during my master's, and we slow-danced to every song until the singles looking to mingle were sick to death of our cuteness.

In the morning, we slept in, recovering from our mild hangovers. We had to check out by noon, so we had lazy, sleepy sex, making sure to finish by eleven fifty-five. I loved spending the night with Judi – for the all-night cuddles as well as the morning sex – and I wondered why I'd denied myself the pleasure for so long.

She took me to her favorite Chinese restaurant, where she said she'd gone at least once a week during her undergrad. The owners still recognized her, and they insisted on heaping our plates with free spring rolls and peanut sauce.

We strolled through the city hand-in-hand, pointing out places we'd gone and the memories we'd had there. I was surprised to find out she'd gone to one of my favorite parks regularly during the summers. Our time here had overlapped, so there was a good chance we'd both been in the same park at the same time, yet I'd never seen her.

"And trust me, I would've remembered you," I said.

Around six, we regretfully decided it was time to head back to Fronton. I took the wheel since Judi had driven on the way here. We turned on a playlist she'd made of chill indie pop and hit the highway, her hand-feeding me snacks every few minutes.

"This was an amazing weekend," I told her. "It was so sweet of you to plan this for me."

"I'm glad you enjoyed it," she said. "I knew you'd never say you wanted to do anything for Valentine's, but that you'd love it if I surprised you with something."

"Is that what you were thinking?" I asked with a laugh. "I'd been assuming we were on the same page about Valentine's being stupid."

She turned sharply toward me. "Stupid?"

"Don't get me wrong. *This* wasn't stupid," I said, taking my eyes off the road for a millisecond to look at her. "I mean Valentine's in general is a consumerist holiday that corporations came up with in order to sell more stuff." I snorted. "Why else would anyone ever buy heart-shaped chocolate?"

She was quiet, and I started to realize I'd put my foot in my mouth. She'd gone to all this effort to make Valentine's special for me, and in return I'd told her the whole thing was stupid.

"There are heart-shaped chocolates in the back

seat," she said in a small voice. "I was going to give them to you once we got back to Fronton."

I paused to change lanes even though I didn't need to, just to take a moment to get my thoughts together. "I'll eat them. Happily."

"While thinking they're stupid."

"No! I mean…" I wished I wasn't driving so I could hug her. "It doesn't matter what shape they are. It's the thought that counts."

"That's what people say when someone gives them a gift they hate!" She sounded more upset than ever. "Why did you pretend you liked this? Why didn't you say something about hating Valentine's?"

"I did like it," I said. "I don't have to be a fan of the holiday to enjoy spending a night with you in a different city."

"But the dinner," she said. "The romance. You thought all of that was silly."

"Not silly! Just… pointless?" Oh God, I was digging my hole deeper. "I mean, I want to show you I love you every day. I don't need a special occasion for it."

"Because you hate the special occasion."

"No, I don't!" I took a breath, trying to figure out how to explain my feelings without hurting her. She'd put so much effort into making this weekend special, and I'd proceeded to shit all over what she'd done. No wonder she was more sensitive than usual.

"Let's review what happened this weekend," she said. "I want to know what was going on in your head. I came to pick you up at work. You thought we were going to have a normal night, and instead I told you I had a Valentine's surprise. You decided to, what… suffer through it? Go along with it, pretending you liked it, and then tell me afterwards that you hate the entire concept of Valentine's?"

"Not at all." My heart was beating faster. She was seriously pissed off, and I hated it. "I was happy you wanted to do something nice for me. There was nothing more to it than that."

"Look, if you're not into something, you should just tell me," she said tightly. "I'd rather know how you feel, and then I can act accordingly."

"I'm sorry. I didn't want to ruin the weekend by telling you I'm not crazy about Valentine's Day."

"So instead you waited and told me after." She let her head flop against the headrest. "I can't stand being in the dark about things, Ella. This is partly on me for wanting to surprise you rather than asking if you wanted to do anything. But still, I would rather have known how you felt from the start."

"It's not like I was suffering through anything," I said. "I had a good time. I didn't think I was keeping anything from you."

"Just don't do anything like this again, okay?" Her tone was anxious. "Please. Honesty and openness are important in a relationship. I like to be on the same page as my partner, not to have them keeping things from me."

"I understand. I was only trying to make you happy."

"Well, don't!" she said. "That's like some shit a guy would do – telling me little white lies because they think I can't handle the truth. I thought you were better than that."

"I am!"

"Then act like it. If my cooking sucks, tell me. If my butt looks big in my jeans, I want to know. If you want to go out with your friends rather than staying in with me on a Friday night, just fucking say it."

We were quiet for the rest of the drive home.

And when she dropped me off at my place, she didn't give me any chocolates.

*

I couldn't confess to Sam. He'd "helped" more than enough. I couldn't stew in my guilt without telling *somebody* about what was going on, either.

At a loss for what to do, I ended up making a coffee date with my friends for the next afternoon. Deena and Mindy met me at a café – *not* Caffeine Hut – at two PM sharp.

"Hey!" I said, embracing each of them in turn. "How've you been?"

I hadn't seen them since shortly after Judi and I had started dating. We'd been spending so much time together, I'd hardly had time for anyone else. I'd updated my friends via text about our relationship, and they were understanding about not seeing me as much. I'd never planned to be one of those girls who ditched her friends as soon as she started dating someone, but when Judi came into the picture, I couldn't help it.

We ordered lattes and grabbed a table with comfy armchairs. As I settled into my seat, they peppered me with questions about my relationship, which I answered as best as I could. They were more curious than I'd expected, and I ended up having to assure them I'd give them a chance to meet Judi soon. "Then you'll get to judge her for yourselves," I told them.

They caught me up on their own recent adventures – Deena had gone to Texas for a work trip, and Mindy was on again with her off-and-on girlfriend of a few years. I only half-listened, more eager to change the topic back to myself – or rather, to the story I'd concocted.

"Do you remember the Internet post I was telling you about last time I saw you?" I asked, trying to sound casual. "The one about the girl who helped her brother talk to a girl, and then ended up dating her herself?"

Although they didn't look too excited to hear about this random person on the Internet again, they nodded.

"That girl posted an update the other day," I said, leaning toward them. "She's been dating the girl for a couple of months now. Her brother found out, and he ended up being okay with it – but the girl still doesn't know."

"She didn't tell her?" Deena asked.

"She kind of told some half-truths," I said. "She said she gave her brother advice on how to talk to her, not that she was the one actually doing the talking."

"That's not so bad," Mindy said. "That's pretty close to being honest."

"I thought so, too," I said. "But then the girlfriend freaked out over another tiny thing – not even a lie. She said she wanted complete honesty in a relationship, and nothing less."

"That's just silly," Deena said, frowning. "No one can be totally honest all the time. What about those white lies people tell? Like saying someone looks nice in their outfit even if they don't?"

"She – this girl, I mean – actually used that as an example." I curled my fingers around my latte. "She doesn't want any lies between them at all."

"People lie all the time," Mindy said. "I lie to Georgia. Just this morning, I told her I was going to work instead of saying I was meeting you."

Georgia was constantly jealous of Mindy, especially her close friendship with Deena. Sometimes I wondered if there was something to that, actually, so I couldn't blame her.

"I don't know if that's a great example of a healthy relationship," I said. "How many times have you two broken up, again?"

"Four," she said, and grinned sheepishly. "Since the new year."

"You two don't lie to me, do you?" Deena asked. "Wait, are you lying to me right now?"

Mindy giggled, and I forced a laugh as the conversation devolved into jokes about lying to each other. I couldn't bring it back to the topic I wanted to talk about without confessing that I'd been talking about myself the whole time.

Now that I thought about it, I *was* lying to them right now. I seemed to be doing that a lot lately, and I didn't like it.

They seemed to think hiding the full truth from Judi was no big deal, though, and I figured that was what I should do.

Even if a small voice at the back of my mind told me everything was going to go horribly wrong.

TWENTY – JUDI

Now that we'd been official for a week, it was time for me to meet Ella's family. In my mind, it was no big deal. I already knew her brother, after all.

It seemed to be a bigger deal for her. I harassed her all week to let me come over on Friday, and she only reluctantly agreed. She kept saying things like "it'll be weird" and "it's still so soon" until she finally gave in.

I was curious to meet her mom and little sister, but honestly, the main reason I was pushing for this was to get seeing Sam out of the way. The time we'd run into him at the winter market didn't count.

If Ella and I were to get more serious, if I was to eventually become part of her family, I'd have to see him from time to time. The longer I dated Ella without speaking to him in person, the more awkward it was going to be when I did.

In the end, we agreed that I'd come over so we could hang out at her place instead of mine. It wasn't going to be a big, fancy meet-the-family scenario. Sam, Coco, and Ella's mom would be around, and we could talk to them as much or as little as we wished. If we felt like having some privacy, we could always go in her room.

"Although I don't think we should… be intimate," she told me over the phone on Thursday night. "If they hear the slightest sign of it, they'll never let me live it down."

"That's okay," I said. "I can always bring you over to my place afterwards so I can ravish you."

When the time came, I drove over to her place with a bottle of wine I'd picked up and some coloring books for Coco. I wanted to make a good impression, even if this wasn't an "official" meeting.

As soon as the door swung open, I realized I probably shouldn't have worried. A woman I had to assume was Ella's mom wrapped me in a rib-crushing hug, not letting me go until I squeaked for mercy. "I'm Fran," she said.

"Are you Judi?" a little girl in a pink tutu asked, peering up at me. "You're pretty!"

Not quite knowing how to respond, I looked around helplessly for Ella. The TV blasted a kids' song from the other room, and the smell of baking muffins filled the entryway. This entire house radiated warmth and homeliness. It was nothing like my family's home.

"Excuse my family," Ella said, appearing out of nowhere to take me by the arm. "They're… enthusiastic."

"They're great. I like them." I threw a backward glance over my shoulder as Ella escorted me to the kitchen. They didn't seem like they were going to follow us – for now.

"Have a muffin," Ella said, pulling one out of the tray where they sat cooling on top of the stove.

"Your mom made them?"

"Yeah. Oatmeal chocolate chip." She took a bite, then handed it to me.

"Thanks for getting your germs all over my muffin." I laughed.

"I think you can handle them. You get a lot more germs from me every time we kiss… or…" She waggled her eyebrows.

A cough came from the door, where Fran stood shaking her head. "I'm going to pretend I didn't hear that. Would you girls like the TV? I can get Coco to play somewhere else."

"I want to play with Judi," Coco shouted from the other room.

I glanced at Ella, feeling slightly overwhelmed. "I'll pour us a glass of wine, and then we'll play with Coco."

"Great!" Fran said. "I'll let Sam know you're here."

My stomach churned at the thought of seeing him again. This was what I'd wanted, and yet now that I was here, coming here seemed like such a strange thing to do. I could've waited to meet the family, I could've put this off a while longer…

But no. It would be better to get this over with. And Sam was a nice guy – he wouldn't make this *too* weird.

Ella and I headed into the living room with our wine and our muffins. Coco had a kids' show blaring on the TV. As the cartoons broke into song and dance, she spun along with them, belting out the words as her pink tutu flew around her legs.

"How can I play with you?" I asked when her performance came to an end. "I don't know these songs."

"Sing them anyway!" she said, grabbing my hands. "Spin with me!"

I glanced at Ella, who gave me a quick nod. I spun in a circle with Coco, trying to keep up with her until she suddenly flopped to the floor. "Whoo!" she yelled. "That was awesome! Ready to do it again?"

"Hey, Judi." A familiar voice came from the door.

I got up quickly, dusting off my knees. "Hey, Sam. How's it going?"

"I never thought I'd find you in my living room playing with my kid sister," he said with a wry smile. "Actually, I hoped I would, but…"

But as his girlfriend, not his sister's. I cut him off, wanting to nip the weirdness in the bud.

"It's good to see you. The new job's going good?"

"It's fine," he said. "Better than Caffeine Hut, anyway. How's Wren and everyone?"

"Not too bad. We got a new regular who's almost as crazy as Jacob."

"Why, what's he do?"

"He comes in, buys one coffee, and spends half the morning scribbling in a notebook and staring at people," I said. "We're thinking about banning him, but he hasn't actually done anything."

We talked a little longer, and I felt myself relaxing. This wasn't so bad after all. Sam was a grown man, and he could be an adult about not getting the girl he'd wanted. I was glad I'd come.

He excused himself, saying he had to make dinner, and I turned back to Ella and Coco. "You didn't take over spinning her?" I asked Ella.

"Nah, none of us do that. Makes us too dizzy."

"Thanks for warning me ahead of time." I rolled my eyes.

"She'll love you forever if you keep spinning her." Ella grinned.

"Yeah, spin me!" Coco said.

I gave in and spun around with her another time. Then I had to pick her up and spin her... and after that, I put her in a chair and spun her.

By the time she was finished spinning, I was amazed she hadn't puked.

"Ella, come help me set the table," Fran called.

As Ella went ahead, Sam came back into the room. Coco sat on the couch with her knees up, playing with the hem of her tutu.

"Hey, I wanted to talk to you privately for a second," Sam said. "I hope you know I'm happy for you and Ella. You two are clearly way better together than we would've been, and there's no hard feelings on my part."

It was a relief to hear that. "That's what I thought, but it's good to hear you say that. I hope we can be friends. I always liked talking to you. It was fun when we were text buddies."

A strange expression crossed his face, one I didn't understand.

At least, I didn't until Coco piped up from the couch. "You were never texting him. You were texting Ella."

I blinked, then blinked again. My mind had suddenly gone blank, and I wasn't sure if I could trust what my ears had just heard. "What?"

"Ignore her," Sam said quickly. "She doesn't know what she's talking about."

Coco looked up from her seat, her small features indignant. "I'm little, not deaf. I was right here when you and Ella planned everything. Even just now, you said you wanted to talk privately, and then you talked right in front of me."

"You – she…" Sam stuttered, looking back and forth between Coco and me.

"Ella even told Sam what to say while you were on a date," Coco said. "She was on the phone, listening to you and texting him."

"What is she talking about?" I asked, my heart hollow. "Ella said you asked her for advice about what to say to me."

"They planned that, too," Coco said in a tattletale tone. "They sat here and decided exactly what to tell you."

The blood drained from my face. I turned toward Sam, hoping he could explain this somehow. Hoping he could tell me it wasn't true.

He plastered a weak smile onto his face. "Silly, isn't it? I was such a loser. I can't believe I ever thought it would be a good idea."

"So you lied to me," I said. "The two of you conspired to lie to me."

His smile faltered. "If you want to put it that way."

My throat was too tight for me to speak. Red flooded my field of vision, staining everything around me. I stood up and headed for the door without another word.

I never wanted to see a single member of this family again.

TWENTY-ONE – ELLA

With the table set, I headed back into the living room to call the others for dinner. Everyone was getting along better than I'd expected – there was barely any weirdness between Judi and Sam, and Coco had instantly taken to Judi. Although I'd spent the week dreading bringing them together, now that it was actually happening, I was actually looking forward to sharing a meal with all of my favorite people.

"Dinner's ready," I sang out – and froze.

Sam was hanging his head, his hands over his face. Coco sat on the couch, kicking the air lazily with a smug expression on her face.

And Judi… Judi was nowhere to be seen.

"Where'd she go?" I asked, my throat tight.

Sam looked at me with anguished eyes. "I'm so sorry, Ella. I never meant her to find out. If I'd had any idea this would happen…"

My stomach knotted up. I didn't have to ask to figure out what he was talking about. "You told her?" I asked, bile rising in my throat.

"No," Sam mumbled. "Coco did."

I looked at my little sister again, noticing the self-satisfaction on her face again. "*You* did this?" I asked. "Why would you do such a thing?"

She laced her fingers in her lap, still twitching her legs. "You thought I didn't know?" she asked. "You always act like I'm not even here. But I am, and I have ears."

"I know you knew," I said, frustrated – even though I hadn't particularly thought about it. "That doesn't mean you were supposed to tell Judi."

"Well, you didn't tell me not to."

Sam came to my side, the two of us facing off against the nine-year-old. "You knew fully well that it was going to bother Judi," he said. "And you did it anyway – to prove a point?"

"If you felt like we were ignoring you, you could've said something about it," I said weakly.

"Instead, you chose to say the one thing that might ruin your sister's relationship," Sam went on. "She's waited her whole life to meet the right girl, and she and Judi are perfect together."

It was nice to know he had my back – even if everything else was falling apart around me.

"Then she shouldn't have lied," Coco said, although the smugness on her face was beginning to falter. "People shouldn't lie."

"Where did you learn that? The Teletubbies?" I asked.

Mom came into the room, her eyes sweeping around to investigate why we hadn't come for dinner. Sam broke down the situation for her, being completely open about everything that had happened from the start.

She put her hand over her heart. "You need to go after her, Ella."

"Right now?"

"Yes. Sam and I will have a talk with Coco." She glanced my now repentant-looking sister. "And when you get back, the three of us will have a talk, ourselves. But for now, you need to catch up with her and see if you can explain things in a way she'll understand."

"You think so?"

She nodded. "You messed up, but this isn't unforgiveable. Not if you ask me."

The only problem was, Judi *hadn't* asked my mother.

Still, I took off like a shot, racing out to my car. As I climbed in, the futility of my task hit me. Judi had a several-minutes head start, not to mention that I didn't actually know where she'd gone. She could be anywhere in this entire city. Hell, she could've left town!

There was a good chance she'd gone to her place, so I headed that way first. It was snowing, the flakes landing wetly on my windshield. I turned on the wipers, chasing the soft flakes away as fast as I could. With panic rising within me, I was in no mood to admire the peaceful blanket of snow that was settling over my surroundings.

I pulled into her driveway and looked around. Her car was nowhere to be seen, although her roommate's was there. Should I go inside and ask Chelle if she might know where Judi was? I decided instead to try another destination.

Judi wasn't at Caffeine Hut, or the pizza place she liked, or the gay-friendly bar where we'd had our first date. I pulled over and took a moment to think about where else she might've gone. I could barely form clear thoughts when my mind was racing all over the place. With every minute that passed, I grew more and more despondent.

I grabbed my phone and tried calling Judi. If she didn't pick up, I'd leave a message. I'd apologize from the bottom of my heart. If she knew, if she understood how this had happened, there was no way she could stay mad at me.

To my surprise, she actually picked up – but she didn't give me any time to make my case. "Ella, I thought you might call," she said coldly. "Do me a favor, and don't bother to call again."

Was she going to hang up just like that? "Wait," I said desperately. "I know I fucked up. At least hear me out."

"I don't know what there is to hear," she said. "You've been dishonest with me since day one. You had every opportunity to tell me the truth, and you didn't. You made me think I had the full story when you were laughing behind my back the whole time. You even plotted with your brother about how to fool me better."

"It wasn't like that," I gasped, my heart wrenching. "I only wanted to help Sam. I know it was dumb. I never thought I'd meet you or fall for you."

"You still don't get it, do you?" Her voice wasn't so cold anymore – it dripped with rage, and I wasn't sure if that was better or worse. "I don't *care* that you pretended to be Sam. I care that you lied about it! We could've laughed about you texting me, the way we laughed about him asking you for advice. But you never let me in on the joke. You decided not to give me a chance. I had to find out the truth from a nine-year-old kid. Do you know how humiliating that was?"

"I only bent the truth so you wouldn't be mad." I stared helplessly at the falling snow beyond my windshield.

"Maybe I would've been mad. But you know what? I wouldn't have broken up with you for it."

"You're not doing that now, are you?" I shriveled against the car seat, waiting with dread for her answer.

She paused for a long moment. "I don't want to, Ella, but you haven't left me a choice. Only a week ago, I was telling you how I can't stand lies. Little white lies are the worst of all. I need to feel like my partner is on my team, and you made me feel the opposite of that. I don't see how I could ever trust you again."

My hand was suddenly too weak to keep the phone against my ear. I brought my knees to my chest so they could hold the phone up. "Please don't," I begged. "Don't do this. I'll be better from now on. I'll never keep anything from you again, I promise."

"The thing is, I already gave you that chance." She sounded sad. She also sounded sure of herself. "I can't be with someone I can't trust. Put yourself in my shoes. I don't think you'd want to continue this relationship, either."

"Yes, I would." This couldn't seriously be happening. A tear fell from my eye, and I didn't bother to wipe it away. "I love you, Judi. You told me you loved me. We can work through this, I swear. I'll do anything."

"It's already past that point. I'm sorry."

"Don't do this. Especially not over the phone. Where are you? I'll come to you – we'll talk about this in person. Please, baby, please."

There was a long pause. I held my breath, hoping – praying – she was about to give in. I knew she loved me, so there was no way she'd drop me like this. She had to give me another chance. *Had* to.

But the only thing I heard next was the dial tone.

TWENTY-TWO – JUDI

Hanging up that phone was the hardest thing I'd ever done in my life. I wiped away the tears I'd been silently shedding and turned to Chelle. "I made the right decision, didn't I?"

"Only you can say whether it was best for you." She gazed at me sympathetically. "Can I get you another glass of wine?"

"No." I sniffled. "I need something more comforting. Something like…" *Like Ella's arms.* "Never mind. No food or drink in the world is going to make me feel better."

"Another blanket, maybe?"

"Okay."

I looked at my phone again as she went to get one out of her room. I was glad I'd parked down the street so Ella wouldn't know I was here. She'd probably come knocking if she knew I was here, and I wasn't sure if I could resist her apologies in person.

I wanted to be with her more than anything. But how could I when she'd betrayed me like that? I kept going over the sequence of events in my mind. How confused I'd been about Sam's two personalities… how things had fallen into place when Ella told me she'd "helped" him. The story had still felt a little off at that point – I should've listened to my intuition.

Why had she never come out and told me she'd been the one texting? I'd been so calm when she'd told me her half-truth. Why had she thought I'd be angry at the other half?

"I don't get it," I said as Chelle wrapped the second blanket around me. "I just don't get it."

"It's okay, honey. You have a lot to process." She nudged me to move to one side, then the other, and pushed the blanket underneath me, tucking me in on the couch. "Do you want to be alone?"

"No, I want to be with her."

"Stay strong." She patted my back. "If this is a dealbreaker for you, then stick to it."

She walked away, only stopping when I spoke. "But *should* it be a dealbreaker?" I asked. "Am I being crazy?"

"You have to pick your own dealbreakers, Judi. I can't do that for you." She hesitated, then pursed her lips. "Call me if you need anything. Anything at all."

I nodded and grabbed a Kleenex as I scrolled upward to the beginning of my conversation with Sam. With Ella posing as Sam, rather.

I reread the first few messages, almost smiling before the pain hit me again. Those days felt so long ago. How had I ever thought these messages could come from Sam? They were so wildly different from the way he spoke and acted in real life. Then once I'd started texting Ella, she'd sounded just like "him."

I scrolled downward, remembering how she and I had forged a friendship over text. Now that I knew the truth, I couldn't even reminisce about it fondly. All I felt was anger about how the two of them had betrayed me.

And then Ella had met me in person, and she'd known who I was. Not right from the start, but now that I thought about it, I could guess the moment when it'd clicked in her mind. I remembered telling her my name wasn't Julie, but Judi with an I. The sick look on her face was imprinted on my mind. How had I not known something was up?

As I thought about it, more and more pieces fell into place. Like how she'd been so standoffish – ending our first couple of dates early, making me think I'd done something wrong. Now I understood.

So many times early on, she'd known things about me that she shouldn't have, or she'd avoided a topic we'd been talking about over text. And then when we ran into Sam, she pretended he was a distant acquaintance. She'd been so quick to deceive me at every possible turn. I couldn't forgive her for that. There was no possible way.

I skimmed through a few more messages, my lips tugging upward despite myself as I reread a witty remark she'd made. No one got my sense of humor like she did. No one shared my interests… no one understood me as a person…

But she didn't understand me that well, or she never would've lied to me like this.

I wiggled around in my blanket. Chelle had wrapped me so tightly, I felt like a bug in a rug. I could've gotten up, but I opted to call out to her instead. "Chelle? I'll take you up on that glass of wine after all."

*

Ella contacted me several times over the next few days. She phoned rather than texting, which I assumed was because texting would've reminded me of why I was mad in the first place. Unluckily for her, no matter what method she used to reach me, there was no way I would or could forget.

She left messages every time she called, which I deleted without listening to. I didn't trust myself to hold strong if I heard her pleading for my forgiveness. I could steel myself against her when I was reading her words on a screen, but if I were to hear her desperate voice, I might've given in.

And I wanted to give in. I wanted that more than anything. Being away from her was miserable, and everyone in my life had been commenting about how down I looked and how quiet I'd been. I missed Ella like a lock might miss its key. It felt wrong to not have her in my life, especially when I knew I could call her anytime and she'd be at my side in ten minutes.

But I couldn't do it. Every time I thought about it, I remembered the lies she'd told – not just one or two, but constant lies from the time we met up to the time she got caught.

If she'd been honest at any point, maybe I could've forgiven her. But she didn't even tell me the truth herself, her little sister did. That was the part that hurt the most.

I almost expected her to come into Caffeine Hut, or to send Sam on her behalf. I bristled at the thought. They'd practically be stalking me if they did that. I composed speeches in my mind where I told them to go away and leave me alone – and I practiced them mentally because I knew I'd never be able to get the words out otherwise.

But it wasn't necessary. Ella never came, and neither did Sam, or any other member of the family. Aside from the phone calls, they were leaving me alone.

As the days ticked by, Ella's calls became less frequent. They came once a day instead of two or three times, and then a whole day went by without a call.

She seemed to be giving up, which was what I wanted. The less she called, the less I'd have to hurt. And yet, the realization that she was giving up pained me, too. If she was really in love with me, wouldn't she try harder than that?

On Thursday, almost a full two weeks had passed since our break-up. I'd have to see Ella at the Pride committee meeting tomorrow. I sat on my bed, knees to my chest, and thought about not going. I couldn't deal with seeing her. Even now that a little time had passed, the wound was still as fresh as ever. Seeing her in person, having her try to talk to me, would cut me open again. Maybe even deeper than before.

I'd made a commitment to the Pride festival, though. It was bigger than either of us, bigger than our relationship. Another member of the marketing subcommittee had stopped showing up recently, and our responsibilities were growing as we got closer to the festival. The group needed me.

My phone lit up with a call from Ella, and I collapsed onto my back as I let it ring. There was a good chance that she was also conscious that she'd see me tomorrow. At this point, she'd probably figured out I wasn't going to take her back, and she was just calling to ask if we could be civil to each other at the meeting. Still, I let it ring, and when the phone beeped to indicate there was a new voicemail, I deleted it without listening. Again.

I opened Facebook Messenger and found my conversation with Ian. *Hey,* I wrote. *Going to the meeting tomorrow?*

I rolled onto my side and pressed my face into the pillow as I waited for his reply. My phone dinged a minute later.

Of course. Aren't you? he asked.

I held my thumb above my phone screen, hesitating as I debated how to reply. *I am,* I finally said. *I was just wondering because I could use your help. I need some distance between me and Ella. Could you make sure to sit between us?*

Now his response was instant. *Why? She's too hot to handle? Can't control yourself when she's around?*

Not exactly, I wrote. *We split up, and we're not exactly on good terms at the moment. Although she'd like to be, if you know what I mean.*

Somehow his next reply came even faster than the last one. *Really?!?!?*

The next few messages came in a rapid torrent. *I'm so sorry to hear that!*

I really thought you two were in it for the long haul.

What happened?

You don't have to tell me if you don't want to.

But seriously, so sorry!

I might've laughed if I hadn't been so close to crying. *I'll explain everything later,* I told him. *Not quite up for it at the moment. I just need you to be a buffer between us.*

I'll buffer like a YouTube video! he wrote. *For real, I'm here for you for whatever you need. Just let me know.*

Thank you, I wrote.

But there was nothing he could do about this hole in my heart.

Twenty-Three – Ella

If the Pride meeting had been anywhere other than my own library, I might not have gone. I already knew what I needed to do in terms of fundraising, and I could just update my subcommittee by email if I wanted to.

But the meeting was right down the hall from the desk where I'd spent most of the day. I would've had to slink by, passing it on my way to the front door. I would've been more ashamed of myself for skipping the meeting than for going.

Or maybe I was just dying to see Judi.

I missed her. Her eyes, her voice, her hair, her face. I missed her serious debates and her teasing jokes. I even missed all the little things she did that annoyed me.

I'd spent two straight weeks thinking about her every moment. I'd gone over and over what'd happened, remembering each step in the sequence that brought us to this point, and contemplating all the times I could've done something differently so that we would still be together.

If I could see her again, maybe I could convince her to hear me out. And if not, at least I'd get to be in her presence for a little while. That might be the best I could get, and even if it wasn't much, I'd take it. At least it'd be better than getting none of her at all.

So I made my way to the boardroom a few minutes past the hour, showing up intentionally late so there'd be no chance of drama between us before the meeting. My eyes instinctively went to the spot where she usually sat. Ian was in her place, and he gave me a sympathetic look. My gut wrenched – had Judi not come? I glanced to the seat next to Ian, and she was there.

Now I understood. She'd positioned him between us purposely. She didn't want to be anywhere near me.

I dropped into my seat, earning an annoyed glance from Todd at the head of the table. "If we could all try to be on time from now on…"

"Right," I said. "I'm sorry."

I snuck a peek over at Judi as I opened my notebook. She looked even more gorgeous than she had in my memory – two weeks had been long enough to make me forget exactly how attractive she was. Her lips were fuller, her eyes were bluer – but her face showed no hint of the constant, slightly amused smile that had made me fall for her in the first place. Had it disappeared because of me?

As Todd concluded his introduction and we broke into our subcommittees, I kept glancing over at Judi from time to time – so much that she must've felt my gaze on her. I would've thought she'd look at me sometimes, even if just by coincidence, and yet I never caught her looking at me once. She must've been making a real effort to *not* look my way.

When the meeting ended, I tried once more to catch her eye. She kept her head low as she packed up her stuff. She'd never look at me if I didn't force her hand.

I couldn't take this anymore. "Judi, would you talk to me for one minute?" I asked, my voice barely a whisper. "Just one minute. That's all I ask."

Ian stood, shielding her as if she needed protection. From *me.* "Judi doesn't want to talk to you right now," he told me.

I stared at him. We'd known each other for years, and he was acting like I was a stranger. "She can speak for herself, can't she?"

"She doesn't want to speak to you," he said.

"No, Ian, it's okay." Judi squeezed his arm. "You've been amazing, but I think it might be best if I do talk to Ella. Only for a minute."

"You have sixty seconds," he said, looking at his watch as he backed a few feet away. "If she's upset after this, Ella, I swear to God…"

"Let us talk!" I snapped, then turned to Judi. Her eyes were wide, her lips a thin line. I wanted so badly to hold her and comfort her, but if I were to touch her right now, it'd do the exact opposite. "Look, I don't know if you've been getting my messages."

"I haven't."

"I want you to know how truly, deeply sorry I am. I never meant to hurt you at all. When I started messaging you, I liked you more than I ever expected. I forgot it was even supposed to be for Sam. I was already falling for you before I ever met you, before I even knew what you looked like. I kept trying to think of ways that I could keep talking to you even if things didn't work out between you and my brother."

"And?" She licked her lips, her expression unchanged.

Only two weeks ago, I would've had the right to lean in and kiss those perfect lips. I would've been able to press myself against her and feel every curve of her body. The world would've melted around us, and all our problems would've gotten better. But I'd lost the right to do any of that. She was off-limits to me now, and if I couldn't convince her to take me back, she always would be.

"Ten more seconds," Ian said.

I spoke faster, my words blending into each other in my rush to get them all out. "I love you, Judi. The kind of connection we have doesn't come along every day. I can't apologize enough for being dishonest with you. If you give me another chance – "

"Time's up." Ian stepped toward us. "Or did you want to give her more time, Judi, honey?"

She hesitated, her eyes searching mine. I didn't know what she was looking for, but I looked straight back at her, begging her silently to accept my apology. I didn't want to go on without her. I couldn't.

"No," she finally said. Her eyes stayed on mine, holding me transfixed in her gaze.

"No?" I whispered.

Slowly, she shook her head. "No, Ella. I'm done."

*

She was done. The words echoed in my mind as I drove home, my heart hollow. They stayed there as I shook my head silently at Sam's questioning glance, and as Mom quietly turned away from Coco.

I still thought about Judi as I went to work the next day and came home. When I went out with my friends, when I lay in bed at night, she was on my mind. Always.

I didn't call her again. That would've been too pushy of me. She'd told me how she felt, and if I were to keep going after that, I would've been asking for a restraining order. Things weren't meant to be for us, and I had to accept that.

Even if they *would've* been meant to be if I hadn't so completely fucked up.

"It's not your fault," I told Sam, who'd been apologizing nonstop since the break-up. "It's mine. I agreed to text her and help you. You just had the idea – I went through with it. And I'm the one who kept it from her for so long, even though I was in a relationship with her."

"I know, but I can't help but blame myself. If I hadn't gone to you, you would've met Judi and dated her without any issues."

"Look, you're my little brother. I love that you come to me for help. I never want you to stop." I paused and made a face. "Just, maybe not for help about girls."

"I definitely won't!"

Later, Mom had a talk with Coco, as she'd promised. I didn't know exactly what she said, but a day afterwards, Coco came to me with a downcast look. "I'm sorry I told Judi what you did," she said. "I only did it because I was mad. I didn't know she'd break up with you or that you'd be sad. I want you to be happy again, Ella."

I gave her a hug and told her it was okay. "If it wasn't you, she would've found out some other way. Lying will do that to you."

During Mom's talk with me and Sam, she told us she didn't appreciate our dishonesty and we should've known nothing good would come from this situation. She thought she'd raised us to be smarter than that.

If she hoped to give us any fresh insights, she failed. All we did was nod along and say, "Yes. You're right. I already know."

Another week passed, and it was time for the Pride planning meeting. I showed up, as usual. I pulled my chair closer to my subcommittee's group, farther away from Judi. I focused on what they were saying about our fundraising efforts.

And I tried my hardest not to look her way.

TWENTY-FOUR – JUDI

Ella was leaving me alone, which was great. Really great. So what if she'd left a massive hole in my heart that no amount of wine could fill?

She'd hurt me, and I wasn't going to run back to someone who could put me through that much pain. We'd only dated for a couple of months, only been official for a week. I should be over her soon.

And yet, even after a month had gone by, I definitely wasn't.

"Are you still moping over that girl?" Chelle asked one night after I said no to going out with her and Sabrina. "You need to stop thinking about her. You broke up with her, remember?"

"All too well," I groaned, lying back on the couch and pulling the blanket over me. "This would've been easier if she'd broken up with me. That way I'd be able to move on, rather than constantly second-guessing whether I did the right thing."

"Come out and meet some new people," she urged. "Once you get a new crush, you'll be like, 'Ella who?'"

I chuckled. "Not likely." Ella had blown my mind in more ways than one. Even if I never spoke to her again, even if everyone around me forgot she'd ever existed, she'd left an indelible impression on me. I could never, ever forget her.

"Judi…" Chelle perched on the edge of the couch, next to my thighs. "I'm sick of seeing you like this. Spring has sprung. The weather's finally getting nice. I want to enjoy this time of year, and frankly, you're bringing me down."

"Sorry I can't choose my emotions," I snarked. "I'll go lock myself in my room so I won't depress you anymore."

"Come on. You know that's not what I'm saying." She squeezed my shoulder. "I'd like you to come out and have a good time tonight – or at least try. Please?"

I rolled onto my side, facing the wall. "I'm not up for it. I'm sorry."

I had big plans tonight… with myself. I intended to curl up with some chamomile tea and watch a history documentary. The kind of doc that Ella would've loved, if she'd been here to watch it with me.

"All right, I guess." Chelle's voice was filled with frustration. "Suit yourself – but whenever you're up for acting like yourself again, I'll be here."

I let out a sigh. I hated disappointing her. She was one of my best friends. But I couldn't snap my fingers and feel better about the whole Ella thing. It just wasn't possible.

"You know, if you're still feeling this bad about

the break-up now that a whole month has passed, maybe you really loved her," Chelle said quietly.

I tensed up. "Of course I really loved her," I snapped. "That was never the question. Have you listened to me talk about this relationship at all? The issue was that she lied to me from day one. How could I ever trust her again?" My voice rose. "What else would she lie to me about?"

"Whoa, chill out," Chelle said. "I'm not the one who hurt you."

That was true. Ella was.

And that was why I couldn't take her back.

*

As March turned to April, my feelings for Ella didn't fade. The only thing that changed was that people asked me about her less. My friends and family seemed to have accepted that this grouchy, sulky Judi was the new me. It was as if they'd forgotten the different person I'd been when I was with her. The different person I could still be.

I tried to get her off my mind, and sometimes I even came close. Once, a cute customer flirted with me at the coffee shop, and I almost – but didn't – give him my number. Another time, Ian tried to talk me into a blind date with a cute single lesbian he'd encountered. I considered it for a while, but ultimately told him no.

I couldn't forget Ella completely when I still had to see her every other week. Even if I avoided looking at her at the meetings, I could see her in my peripheral vision. Sometimes I even caught a whiff of her floral scent. Every time, my heart grew heavy. It didn't feel right to be in the same room with her and to not have her in my arms.

Ian had supported me through the break-up without even knowing what'd happened, and when I'd told him the details, he was on my side. Now that she'd accepted the split, he'd gone back to being friends with her.

I couldn't say anything about it – he shouldn't have to choose between us, especially when he'd known us both separately before we'd dated. Still, it made me uncomfortable. He might've been sneakily telling her some of the things I said, the same way he occasionally dropped tidbits about her when he spoke to me.

"Ella's going to Denver this weekend," he said casually one Friday, as if the sound of her name didn't stab me straight in the soul. "Didn't you two go there once?"

Only for the most magical weekend ever. "Um, yeah," I mumbled. "We did."

Who was she going there with? What was she going to do there? Would she spend her entire time there thinking about me, the way I would've if I went?

I wanted to know everything about her trip, but... *You're the one who broke up with her, Judi.* I forced a smile and changed the subject.

One of these days, he'd tell me she was dating someone else. I knew that was coming. When someone was as beautiful as her, with such an incredible personality, they wouldn't stay single for long. I might've been Ella's first relationship, but I wouldn't be her last. And because Ian clearly had no idea how intense our relationship had been – how deeply I'd fallen for her in the short time that we'd dated – he'd have no qualms about telling me.

Sometimes it felt like the world was conspiring to push Ella in my face. As soon as one Pride meeting began, Todd directed our attention toward her. "Let's all give Ella a hand," he said. "She's contacted over fifty companies in the area, of which more than ten have agreed to donate. Today she got our biggest donation yet – ten thousand dollars from Ranford Bank. That will pay for the stage, tents, speakers, and stereo equipment all by itself!"

Everyone applauded, yelling out compliments to Ella about how awesome she was. I sank down in my chair, lightly tapping my hands together, looking anywhere but at Ella.

Calling that many companies had taken a lot of time, determination, and bravery – not to mention the persistence and persuasiveness it must've taken to talk them into actually donating. I hoped she knew my weak hand claps were sincere – that I really was impressed by her accomplishment.

She'd done a great job. She *was* awesome.

But the good things about her didn't outweigh the bad… did they?

Twenty-Five – Ella

Life had to go on without Judi. As miserable as I was, the world didn't stop turning because my heart was broken. I still had to go to work every day. Still had to eat, sleep, and drink water. And although it was hard, as the weeks passed it became a little easier.

Over and over, I thought through what'd happened between me and Judi, and why. I sifted through the thoughts until my disappointment and hurt went away and I could look at the situation clear-eyed.

I'd fucked up by being dishonest. I'd kept telling myself it wasn't a big deal when the whole time, I'd known it was. But I kept lying anyway out of my desire to avoid conflict. My obligation to Sam conflicted with my obligation to Judi, and instead of facing that clash head-on, I tried to pretend it didn't exist.

Now honesty became my new policy. I told library patrons who wanted an obscure book that we were never going to order it and that they'd be better off getting it from Amazon. Before, I would've hemmed and hawed around the issue, making them think they had a chance rather than giving a flat-out "no."

I told Sam he was being a dipshit when he described how he was coasting by at work and letting his female colleagues carry him. I told the waitress at a restaurant that my chicken was undercooked and requested a new one. I even told my boss I'd gotten to work late instead of pretending I'd been on time.

The more honest I was, the better I felt. I never had to worry about being caught out or contradicting myself. And even my smallest white lies, the ones I'd barely thought twice about telling, had weighed on me. Now my conscience was clear.

Before, I'd worried that honesty could hurt people. The longer I strove to be honest at all times, the more I saw that was false. Being truthful didn't mean being rude or abrupt. As long as I delivered the truth gently and thoughtfully, people took it better than I expected. And as time went on, they got used to knowing they could expect the full and complete truth from me.

I'd never thought little white lies could hurt anyone, and I still wasn't convinced they didn't have their place. But small lies could turn into big ones, and I wasn't willing to take that chance anymore. Maybe with strangers, but not my family and close friends. I valued those relationships far too much to risk losing them.

The only bad thing was that I'd learned this lesson too late. I'd thought telling Judi the truth would ruin everything, and my lies ruined things instead. I'd lost the woman I valued more than anything, and there was no way for me to undo that. I kept thinking back to the early days of our relationship, contemplating all the times I could've opened up about what I'd done, all the times I'd chosen to hide the truth instead. If I could go back, I'd do everything completely differently.

But it wasn't possible to turn back time.

Never had been, never would be.

I'd made mistakes, and I had to live with them. My only comfort was that at least I'd learned from them.

*

As time went by, I began to think about dating again. Or rather, I began to give in to Deena and Mindy, who were constantly harassing me to give online dating a try.

I'd been so happy with Judi. Happier than I'd been in my life… happier than I'd even imagined. Being with her had felt easy and natural, and I was pretty sure she'd felt the same way. I'd seen how wonderful being part of a couple could be, and I longed to feel that way again. Preferably with Judi, but since she wouldn't give me another chance, it'd have to be with somebody else.

I was still scared that I'd fuck up again and do something terrible to drive a new girl away. But

I was a better person now than I was when I'd met Judi, and now I knew how much love I had to give. I was getting tired of keeping all that love to myself.

"I think I'm ready," I told my friends one night in mid-May over drinks at our usual spot. "You two are going to have to show me how it's done." I set my phone on the table.

"We can make you a TruLuv account?" Deena squealed.

Somberly, I nodded.

"Show some enthusiasm," Mindy said, grabbing my phone. "This is the best possible way to find a girlfriend these days. I know so many couples who've met on TruLuv. You'll be in a relationship in no time."

"I doubt that," I said. "I'll probably get a date or two, at best. Don't all the girls on these apps live in Denver, anyway? They're not going to want to come out here and see me."

"Not with that attitude, they won't." Deena rolled her eyes.

Mindy was busy setting up a profile for me. "Okay, I know your name, obviously. And you're a woman seeking a woman. Let's pick some pictures for you. And how would you describe yourself?"

I sighed. "Nerdy librarian, homebody, still broken-hearted over her last short-term relationship…"

Deena coughed. "You *were* off to a good start. Try again."

"Um… nerdy librarian… wears glasses…"

"Wearing glasses isn't a personality trait," Mindy said. "Sell yourself!"

"I don't know!" I said. "I feel like I'm writing a resume or something."

"You are," she said. "You're trying to get hired for the role of 'girlfriend.'"

But the only girlfriend I wanted was Judi. I sighed again, harder this time. "Can't you write it for me?"

She huffed, but bent over the phone and conferred with Deena in low tones for a minute. I sipped my beer and waited, wondering how long they were going to take.

In no time at all, they looked up and pushed the phone back over to me. "What do you think of this?" Mindy asked.

Seeking the real thing, and nothing less. Smart and funny – I won't admit it, but my friends will tell you. Sweet, caring, and considerate – and surprisingly passionate too. I work as a librarian, but I'm so much more than books. Hoping to find someone I can share my life with. When I fall, I fall hard! Could you be the one that I fall for?

I blinked. "I don't know about this. It doesn't sound like me."

"It's exactly you," Deena said. "I'm going to post

it."

"Wait, no." I reached for the phone. "Wait… just the 'passionate' part – I don't want people to get the wrong idea…"

"Too late," she said. "It's done. Oh, look at this! There's another user just a few miles from here. So much for having to get girls to drive down from Denver."

"Let's check her out," Mindy said. "She could be *the one*."

She leaned over Deena's shoulder and tapped on the screen. Immediately, both of their expressions turned to horror. "Never mind," Deena said, quickly turning off the phone screen. "Denver's not so far. I used to go up there for dates all the time."

"Why are you acting like that?" I asked. "What is it?"

We had a quick struggle for the phone, and finally it landed in my lap. I turned the screen back on, even though I already had an idea of what they might've seen. There was only one profile that would've made them react like that.

My heart clenched into a tight fist as Judi's face filled the display.

What was she doing on a dating app? Had she been so quick to move on? Was she meeting girls? Dating them? Did she have a new partner now? Did she even remember my name?

"Are you okay, Ella?" Mindy asked softly. "You look like you're about to be sick."

"I'm fine," I gritted out. "Just... delete my profile. Delete everything. I don't think I'm ready to date again after all."

Twenty-Six – Judi

My phone vibrated in my apron as I handed a latte to a customer. The coffee shop was slow enough that I took a minute to check the message. I didn't know who would be texting me right now. I didn't get a lot of texts lately – not since I broke up with Ella.

As it turned out, there was no text. The alert was because someone matching my criteria had just signed up on TruLuv. A woman seeking women within a twenty-five mile radius? I clicked eagerly, curious to see how old she was and what she'd written about herself.

A familiar face popped up, and I recoiled as if I'd been punched in the stomach. Ella was trying to meet people on a dating app? Well, good for her. I didn't want her to pursue me forever when I'd clearly told her I wasn't interested. And yet I was physically pained by the thought of her being with someone else.

Before my eyes, the profile disappeared. Had Ella seen me? Had she blocked me?

"You look like your grandma just died," Wren said wryly from behind the cash register. "Wait, no one died, did they? They did, didn't they? I'm sorry!"

"No, no." I cleared my throat. "Clearly I need to

refine my facial expressions. That wasn't the 'someone died' face, it was the 'ex-girlfriend joined a dating app' face."

"Ahh… now I see the difference," she said. "You looked even more miserable than you would've if someone died."

I stashed my phone back in my apron. "It's a weird situation. I mean, I'm on there myself, and yet I'm going to be hurt that she's doing it?"

Chelle had pressured me into making an account a few weeks ago, saying she was sick to death of the funk I was in. Actually, she'd taken my phone and made the account herself. I just hadn't bothered to delete it. I'd gotten a few messages from guys, which were gross enough that I changed my settings to women only. After that, there'd been no messages.

"It's understandable to be hurt," Wren said. "You still want to be with her."

"What? No, I don't." I crossed my arms. "I mean, I *would*, but not after what she did."

"Right, because her lying to you outweighed all the good things about her." Wren gave me a questioning look.

"Yeah." My voice faltered.

"And that's why you're still in love with her after almost two months. Because she was such a horrible person."

"She's an amazing person who did a horrible

thing," I said. "Was I supposed to just say 'okay' and forget about it?"

"No, of course not." She trailed off, giving me a hard stare.

"I sense there's a 'but' coming."

"But you didn't even give her a chance to make things right." She crossed her arms, too, mirroring me. "The way you tell it, you cut her off the second you found out she lied. Ever since, you've been brooding over her."

"That *was* her second chance," I said. "She'd already lied to me once, remember?"

"The Valentine's Day thing? That hardy counts." She scoffed. "No one would've told you they hated Valentine's at the moment when you were taking them for a surprise weekend away, and it's not like you gave her a chance to tell you she hated Valentine's beforehand. You sprung a surprise on her, and she was gracious about it. In fact, the way you tell it, she enjoyed everything about the weekend. She just doesn't like the more corporate aspects of V-Day."

She did have a point. In fact, I'd already had similar thoughts. "Still, I told her how I felt about lying, and she did it anyway. She'd been doing it since day one, and she would've kept doing it indefinitely if her little sister hadn't told me the truth." Heat rose to my face. I'd argued this mentally so many times, and yet talking about it in person still stressed me out. "She was conspiring with her brother. She – "

"She messed up," Wren said, holding up a finger. "I'm not denying that. But is she or is she not the girl of your dreams?"

I pursed my lips, unwilling to answer.

"And are you or are you not still in love with her?"

I hung my head.

"Have you heard of *Cyrano de Bergerac*?"

I looked up at her sharply, confused by the change of subject. "Um… vaguely. What is it?"

"It's a movie from 1990. There's an older version too, but the new one is surprisingly better – at least to me. They're both good. Oh, and they're both based on this super-ancient French play by Edmond Rostand. There's also *Roxanne* with Steve Martin, but we don't talk about that one. It's not the same as the original."

"What's your point?"

"Just that it's a great movie." She turned away and started to mop the counter. "You should give it a watch sometime."

*

With nothing to do that weekend, I decided to check out the movie. I downloaded the newer version, partly because it was in color. Old movies weren't really my thing, and I was already going to have to strain my eyes to read the subtitles. I curled up on the living room couch and pressed play.

A few minutes into the movie, I hardly noticed the subtitles anymore – the plot had drawn me in. The main character, Cyrano, was madly in love with his cousin Roxane, but he thought she'd never return his feelings because of his big nose. To be fair, it was pretty funny-looking.

Ah… I saw why Wren had recommended this. Cyrano's friend Christian was also into Roxane, and he asked Cyrano to write letters to help him win her over. This was like the hetero, 19th-century French version of me and Ella's story.

The trick worked, and Roxane got married to Christian. I snorted to myself. At least Ella's plot with Sam hadn't gotten that far!

Christian went off to war, and Cyrano kept writing letters on his behalf. Christian proceeded to die without Roxane finding out he wasn't writing the letters! I was on the edge of my seat as Roxane, heartbroken, proceeded to join a convent. She'd become a nun!

Cyrano visited Roxane every week, just as a friend. This went on for a good amount of time… *fourteen years.* Then one week, he was wounded on his way there. For some reason – the freaking idiot! – he continued on his way and went to see Roxane rather than seeking medical help.

Somehow in the course of their conversation, the

topic of Christian's last letter to her came up, and he quoted it word for word. This was it… she finally realized it was him who'd written the letters. Him that she'd fallen in love with.

And only then, he showed her his wound… and then he closed his eyes and fucking died!

I let out an exhale I hadn't realized I was holding as the credits began to roll. That movie was infuriating. Cyrano had let the love of his life get away. All he had to do was tell her he was the one writing the letters, and she would've been his. He just had to tell her the truth! She could've left the convent for him, but he let his self-consciousness about his nose get in the way.

Then when she finally found out, it was too late – he was literally dying! They were perfect for each other. Perfect. She wouldn't have cared about his nose, or about anything else. They could've been together, if he hadn't died two minutes later.

Wait… was that why Wren had wanted me to watch this? Was that the message she wanted me to take from it?

Ella and I were perfect together – that much was for sure. And we were both still alive.

Maybe at this point in the story, I wasn't Roxane. I was Cyrano – keeping us from being together for a decidedly silly reason. If I forgave Ella and trusted she wouldn't hurt me again, then we could be together again before one or the other or us was on the verge of death.

Maybe Wren was right. Maybe I'd been stupid to break up with Ella. But at this point, it wasn't like I could just go to her and ask for her back. She was dating now. Besides, I'd pushed her away. I'd been so cold to her at the time of the break-up, ignoring her calls and refusing to talk to her. And I'd cut her off completely for so long.

She'd stopped trying to get me back ages ago. Why would she want to hear from me at all?

I curled into a ball on the couch. She *wouldn't* want to. I'd missed my chance.

Ella was the love of my life, and I was never going to be with her again.

TWENTY-SEVEN – ELLA

Today was the day. All the phone calls I'd made, all the emails I'd written, all the research I'd done and the favors I'd begged were finally going to come to fruition. Everything was culminating in Fronton's first-ever Pride festival.

The sun was shining, and the gentle breeze in the air was welcome as I carried audio equipment from the truck to the stage, helping set things up. Some of the committee members had managed to get some semi-famous local bands to play, and a well-known comedian would be emceeing. The volunteers were the only ones here at this hour, but we buzzed with excitement. Especially me – at least, as long as I didn't accidentally look at Judi.

She was the only not-great thing about the day. I was over her – or I told myself I was – but still, it was hard to see her avoiding my eyes, as if she hated me too much to even look at me. I wished we could be civil toward each other. I would've been her friend if she wouldn't have me as her partner. But she wouldn't even acknowledge I was there.

After setting down an amp with a thud, I turned to Ian. "We're almost done. Looks like we'll be all set up before people start arriving."

He shielded his eyes and pointed into the

distance. "I doubt that. Looks like some are already here."

A gay couple came toward us, holding hands. "This is Pride, isn't it?" one of the men called.

"You're early!" I shouted back. "Come back in a bit!"

The streets had already been blocked off, and a few cops stood in a huddle to one side. Some tents had been erected, and a bunch of vendors were getting ready to display their wares inside. As I looked up at the stage, a rainbow flag unfurled all the way across the front.

My heart swelled. Growing up in this small town, I'd struggled to accept who I was and to find a sense of community with others like me. I'd never once imagined there would be a festival celebrating my sexuality right here in Fronton. I definitely hadn't imagined I'd be an integral part of making it happen.

I let my eyes stray over to Judi, who was placing folding chairs in front of the stage. She paused to look at the flag, and even from a few feet away, I could see she was affected. While we were dating, she'd told me how much this festival meant to her.

She glanced toward me, and my heart stuttered as our eyes met for the first time in months. I chanced a smile – a small one, an apologetic one. She didn't return it.

All right, then. Chastened, I went back to

helping with the stage equipment.

By ten o'clock on the dot, the stage and the vendors were all set up. A few curious onlookers arrived before the emcee even took the stage. There was going to be a full day of music, drag, speeches, and entertainment. The main part of my volunteer work was done. I was still here to help out if anybody needed me, but for the most part, this was my time to relax and enjoy the festival.

I took a seat and watched proudly as the emcee talked about the events we had planned for the day. The only thing that would've made this better was having a girlfriend to share it with. Specifically, Judi. I looked on in pain as a lesbian couple slipped into the seats down the row from me. One put her arm around the other, playing with her hair. Why couldn't that be us?

Stop it, Ella. I'd been looking forward to this day for over half a year, and I wasn't going to ruin it for myself by sulking over my break-up. I pushed my thoughts of Judi into a compartment deep inside myself and sealed it up.

Someone stood beside me, and I pushed my chair back an inch to let them squeeze through. "Not even going to get up for us, Ella?" a familiar voice asked.

I jumped up and wrapped my mom in a hug. "You came!" And so had Sam and Coco.

"Of course we did," Mom said. "We had to see why you've been abandoning us every second

Friday night for months."

"Also, we're really fucking proud of you and all the effort you've put in," Sam said.

"Language!" Mom snapped, covering Coco's ears.

The three of them sat down, and I couldn't keep myself from grinning like an idiot. I laid my head over Mom's shoulder. Even if I didn't have a girlfriend in my life, I still had people who loved, supported, and cared about me.

We watched the bands and entertainment, and when we got hungry around noon, Mom bought us all hot dogs and giant pretzels from one of the vendors. Sam topped things off by getting each of us an iced lemonade. There was a beer tent, too, but we couldn't go in with Coco.

People came and went throughout the day. The turn-out was far better than we'd expected, and the folding chairs weren't nearly enough to contain the crowds. A lot of people ended up voluntarily giving their seats to senior citizens and pregnant women. There seemed to be more people standing than sitting, but nobody complained.

It was a beautiful day, and we were celebrating LGBT rights. It felt like everyone here was in as wonderful a mood as I was.

Around eight o'clock, the official side of the festival wound down. I made my way over to Todd, Ian, and a few of the other volunteers.

"Well, that was a resounding success," I told Todd. "You are so freaking awesome for making this happen."

"I couldn't have done it without you." He patted me on the shoulder, looking as drunk on happiness as I felt. "A few of us are going out for drinks to celebrate. Want to join?"

"To celebrate celebrating? I'm in."

After I said goodbye to my family, the group of us walked over to a bar a few blocks away. Someone had invited Judi, and somehow we fell into step, walking silently side by side. I was aware that, with no more Pride planning meetings for the next few months, I wouldn't see her every other week anymore. In fact, if one of us decided not to volunteer again next year, this could be the last time I saw her at all.

As the group headed into the bar, Judi caught me by the arm. I froze, shocked as much by the feeling of her skin on mine as by the fact that she'd acknowledged my existence. She'd been ignoring me for so long, and I'd assumed it would always be that way.

"I want to talk to you for a moment," she said slowly. The way she dragged her eyes upward to meet mine made me think that maybe earlier, she'd looked away out of fear rather than spite. "Do you – do you think we could do that?"

That's only the one thing I've been dying to do for the past four months. "Sure. Um… what's up?"

Ahead of us, Ian was about to be the last through the door. He turned back and took a look at us, and his eyebrows shot up. "Okay, then. See you inside."

Judi crossed her arms, shivering. She was in tiny denim shorts and a crop top with a rainbow heart on it, which would've been great for the daytime, but now it was getting chilly, especially here in the shade. Still, she looked great. She looked amazing, actually.

"How've you been?" she asked simply, making a face as if to say she knew how strange it was to start a conversation with me this casually. "Are you going to volunteer again next year?"

"I've been good," I said, still awed by the fact that I was actually talking to her. "And yeah, I think I am. What about you?"

"Definitely. This event today… it was like nothing else I've ever seen. I've been to bigger Prides, but seeing this one here, in my own hometown… it was life-affirming. Coming here today was food for my soul."

Only she would describe this that way. The way she worded things always had been quirky and cute, but even so, I found myself agreeing with her completely. "It really was," I said. "I'm so happy we pulled this off."

"And that was largely because of you," she said. I started to wave off the compliment, but she shook her head. "Don't be modest. You know it's true."

"Fine."

I still didn't know why she'd suddenly decided to speak to me. Was this an attempt at friendship? She probably just didn't want to say goodbye forever while we were on bad terms. There was no way she wanted to get back together with me. No possible way.

"I saw you having fun with your family," she said. "I was in and out of the beer tent all day."

Ahh... that explained a little. Now that she said it, I did see a slight glaze over her eyes. Alcohol lowered inhibitions so people could do the things they wanted to do when they were sober. Did that mean she'd been wanting to talk to me?

"I'm glad we emphasized the family-friendly aspect of today," I said. "Coco really enjoyed the kids' stuff."

"Oh, Coco." She looked away as if remembering her last conversation with my sister, then returned her gaze to me. "And your mom and Sam?"

"They liked the music," I said. "I wasn't sure if some of the drag performances would have Mom clutching her pearls, but they kept it reasonably clean."

"Fran doesn't seem like much of a pearl-clutcher."

"She's not. I just thought some of those acts would be seriously scandalous."

Judi chuckled softly. "Give it a few years, and maybe Fronton Pride will be on the same scale as the San Francisco parade. We'll have men walking around in assless chaps and girls wearing nothing but rainbow bikinis."

"We're on the organizing team," I said jokingly. "If that's what we want, we can make it happen."

Was I really joking around again? With *Judi?* I fought the urge to pinch myself. A day or two ago, this would've seemed completely impossible. Even this morning, she wouldn't even return my smile.

"So… TruLuv, huh?" She peered into my eyes.

"Oh God, you saw me."

"There's nothing to be embarrassed about," she said, even though she looked embarrassed. "I'm on there, too."

"I was only on it for about three minutes, and then…"

"And then you saw me?"

I cringed. *Tell her that's not the reason. Tell her it had nothing to do with her.* But no, that wasn't me anymore. If there was ever a time for absolute honesty, it was this conversation. "Exactly."

"I didn't get much use out of it, either. I haven't been dating at all, actually."

A wave of relief went through me. I hadn't realized how much the thought of her dating disturbed me. "Me either," I said. "I've had other things on my mind." *Like you,* I added silently – and it wasn't a lie of omission, because I was pretty sure she could read it on my face.

"It's hard to meet people," she said enigmatically.

I hesitated, then forged ahead. "I think if I did meet someone, I'd be ready. I've been working on myself, and I feel much more ready for a relationship. I wouldn't make any of the newbie mistakes that I made... with you. I've been prioritizing honesty, and it's really working for me."

She looked down. "I'm glad to hear that. For what it's worth, I've realized I overreacted to your mistakes. I never gave you a chance to make things right, and I threw out an amazing relationship that probably could've been salvaged."

A spark of hope lit up in my heart. Was she saying she still had feelings for me? I licked my lips, trying to steady my nerves. *Honesty, always. Just ask her if you want to know.* "Are you saying you still have feelings for me?"

She combed her fingers through her hair, looking forlorn. "I always did, Ella. That was never the issue."

"So..." I trailed off, not wanting to jump to the conclusion that she seemed to be implying.

"I convinced myself that what you did

outweighed all the wonderful things about you," she said. "I thought I could find the same connection we had with someone who wouldn't lie to me. Now that I've had four months to look back on our relationship, I've realized it's rare to find someone who fits me like you do. It may actually be impossible to find someone as perfect for me as you."

Oh my God. Oh my *God*. She really was saying what I thought she was saying.

"And my expectations for you were far too high," she said. "Anyone would've told a white lie and not mentioned they hated Valentine's Day. You were trying to be nice. And as for the other lie… I can't say I understand why you did it, but I think I was too quick to decide it was a dealbreaker. Our relationship was worth more than that."

"I did it because I was terrified to lose you," I said softly. "Great plan, right?"

"Oh, Ella."

She stepped toward me as if she wanted to hug me, then hesitated. With joy swelling in my heart, I closed the distance between us and captured her in my arms. It felt so right to embrace her, her strawberry scent filling my nose. I was holding her again, just the way I'd dreamed of for four months.

"I'm sorry," I said, pressing my face into her shoulder. "I was stupid."

"*I* was stupid." She tightened her arms around my back. "I'd like to try again, if you're willing. We don't have to jump into anything…"

"Oh, we can jump into everything."

Her laugh ruffled my hair. "I mean, we don't have to make things official right away. We can go on a date or two, see if the connection is still there. We spent time apart, and like you said, we've changed."

"Not that damn much." I squeezed her as tight as I could. "I'd make you my girlfriend again right now, if you'd let me."

"You're not mad at me for being so awful for you for so long?" she asked. "I'd understand if you needed to rebuild your trust in me."

I would've wanted to be with her even if she'd ignored me for a year… or ten. She was the one for me. "I betrayed you, you betrayed me. Let's consider it even."

"I'm so glad we could figure this out before one of us dies," she said, almost like she was talking to herself. "Wait, you're not mortally wounded, are you?"

"What? No."

"Good." She ran her fingers through my hair, caressing me as she looked into my eyes. "I'm Cyrano."

"What are you talking about?" I shook my head.

Judi was a mystery, and I intended to spend the

rest of my life figuring her out. Right now, though, there was one thing that was more urgent.

"Never mind," I said. "Kiss me."

TWENTY-EIGHT – JUDI

I walked into the bar, one hand in Ella's back pocket. Todd, Ian, and the other Pride volunteers had taken up a long table at the back of the room. Their animated discussions came to a stop as, one by one, they noticed us coming toward them.

"Is this what I think it is?" Ian screeched.

Expectant faces waited for our answer, making me self-conscious. Ian was the only one who knew the full history of our relationship, but now I saw the rest of the group had been somewhat aware of what happened, too. And by the looks of it, they'd been rooting for us to get back together.

"Maybe," I said, unsure if Ella wanted to keep things private for now.

"If you're asking if we're a couple again, the answer is yes," she said. "And I couldn't be happier."

Heat rose to my cheeks. This had all happened so fast… and yet in a sense, it'd been coming since the day we broke up. The wound she'd given me had slowly healed, and if anything, the distance I'd placed between us had made me appreciate her more than ever before. I loved this woman, completely and whole-heartedly, and that wasn't going to change anytime soon.

Someone said "aww," and someone else clapped. More scattered applause went around the table, and then Todd stood up to clap both of us on the back. "This calls for a drink!"

He insisted on buying us each a beer. After that, the attention faded from us, for which I was glad. There were plenty of things from the day to talk about – although personally, I just sat in my seat, sipping my drink and enjoying the feel of Ella's hand on my leg.

The beers I'd had through the day had left me pleasantly warm, and now I was more content than ever. The part of me that had been missing for so long had returned, making me feel whole for the first time in months. And all it had taken was opening my heart to let Ella back in.

On her part, she'd been ready. I would've thought I'd have to fight for her, to prove that I truly wanted to be with her and that I'd never dump her like this again. But it hadn't even been necessary. It seemed like she'd been waiting for me all this time, like she'd been unable to move on, hoping that I would come back to her.

I guessed that was how it worked when two people were meant to be.

We stayed for a while, celebrating how well Pride had gone. After half an hour or so, though, Ella raked my thigh with her fingernails, and I glanced over to find a meaningful look in her eyes. I remembered that look from before. It usually meant I was in for a whole lot of orgasms.

I gave her a subtle nod. That kiss from before hadn't nearly been enough.

"I think we're going to get going," I said, faking a yawn. "I'm pretty tired. Have fun, everyone!"

"Oh, you're *tired?*" Ian asked, smirking hard. "You're going home to *sleep?*"

"Yes." I shot him a glare, all too conscious of Ella's body heat at my side.

"I'm sure that's *all* you're going to be doing," he said.

"Shut up, Ian." Squeezing by me, Ella swatted his shoulder. "Enjoy the rest of your night, team."

"You to-o-o!" Ian sang out.

We walked back, past the intersection where the festival had been. It was open to traffic again, and cars sped through as if nothing had happened here. I caught sight of a rainbow sticker on the ground, and my heart swelled. What we'd accomplished today did have lasting effects, and those would grow even more as we kept putting on Pride events year after year.

My place was walking distance from here, which was perfect since that last beer had me stumbling. I held onto Ella's arm, partly for support and partly just because I wanted to. I'd been away from her for so long, I never wanted to let go of her again.

We stumbled together as we finally made it through my front door. Then she was on me, her lips leaving my senses tingling. I grabbed at her, my need for her rising more and more urgently. As we kissed, she backed up, hitting the front hallway's wall. We laughed together and went the other way until I slammed into the other wall.

Drunk on alcohol and intoxicated by her presence, I decided to just go with it. I backed her up, little by little, until we staggered into the living room. I kept kissing her, pressing her backwards. The world outside us had vanished – I was immune to everything but her skin, her scent, her lips.

Vaguely, I was conscious of wanting to get her onto the couch. I pointed her toward it blindly, and we fumbled our way there. My legs hit the leather upholstery, and I pulled her down with me.

And collapsed onto already-waiting limbs.

Shrieking, I broke apart from Ella and stood up. The TV was on – I hadn't noticed – and in the dim light, I could see Chelle and Sabrina sitting serenely on the couch.

"You two are in here?" I asked, gasping for breath. "You couldn't have said something before we fell straight on you?"

"You got back with Ella, I see." Chelle popped a

piece of popcorn into her mouth.

"We were watching a movie," Sabrina explained. "But it's fine. We're good with a live lesbian sex show instead."

I recoiled. "Yeah, um, we're going to go. See you two later." I grabbed Ella's hand, tugging her toward the door.

"Pride was amazing, by the way!" Chelle called after us as we went upstairs.

I closed the bedroom door behind us, my face still flushed. "So sorry about them."

"I don't even care." She brushed a strand of hair into her bun, looking adorably shy. "I want you." Her attempt at brazenness made her even cuter.

"And I want you," I said, linking my arms around her neck and breathing in her Ella scent. "You don't know how much I've missed you."

"I think I have an idea." She kissed me, her tongue flicking between my lips and sending a current of heat through my body.

I'd learned my lesson about blindly pushing her around. With my eyes wide open, I led her toward the bed. There were no surprises this time, and we both fell onto it, entangling in a heap of smooth limbs and soft skin.

Straddling her, I kissed my way down her neck and along her collarbone. Her breath came in sharp gasps as I pressed my teeth gently into her clavicle. Desire pooled in my belly, intensifying as I trailed a finger under the collar of her shirt. I grazed a palm over her breast, and I could feel the hardness of her nipple even through the cup of her bra.

"I've been waiting for this for so long," she murmured, and more sparks shot through my body.

"So have I," I said, lifting her shirt over her head. "So have I."

I stripped her down, piece by piece, and she reclined nude before me like a classical woman in a Renaissance painting. Her breasts were ripe and kissable, her stomach curved and soft. I ached to taste her, and after denying myself for so long, I wasn't going to wait a moment longer. Pushing her thighs apart, I dove in between.

I took a moment to appreciate the gorgeousness of her center, her intricate folds already dripping with desire. More than that, I appreciated the fact that she'd allowed me in again. What we were about to do was so intimate, so monumental, and after the way I'd shut her out for so long, I wouldn't have blamed her for not wanting to let me in.

Her eyes met mine as I stroked her thighs. I saw her need for me there... and her trust. Despite what I'd done to her, she somehow still trusted me.

And I wasn't going to let her down – not now, not ever. I grazed my thumb over her clit, still holding eye contact, telling her silently that I loved her.

"*Judi.*" The word slipped out of her in a gasp.

I lowered my head, brought my tongue where my thumb had been. She tasted delectable, and I inhaled the scent of her familiar musk. This, right here – this was where I was supposed to be. I should never have left.

"Oh, yeah." Her hands found the back of my head – I'd forgotten the way she'd always grab me like this, so needy and so shameless. "Right there. Oh… *right there!*"

My tongue played over the patterns that'd become so familiar four months ago. Yet this time, I pleasured her even more enthusiastically than before. This time, I was grateful just to be doing this. In response, her moans were louder, more erotic than ever.

Squeezing her thighs, I licked harder – circle, circle, swirl, swirl. She rose onto her elbows, her hips still shuddering toward me with every stroke of my tongue. "I need more," she breathed. "You know what I need…"

I hummed in response, unwilling to stop using my mouth on her long enough to form words. I brought my tongue lower, to her dripping channel, and delved in as far as it would go. Her legs shook, and she let out a cry.

Her hips rocked up and down, and I hung on tight so I could thrust my tongue into her over and over. She met me each time, matching each thrust with her own. We were in sync, connected – just the way we were supposed to be.

As her cries rose higher and higher, I knew her climax was imminent.

This was the first orgasm I would give her in our new lives together. And we had years – decades – more to come.

TWENTY-NINE – ELLA

I awoke in a tangle of blankets, my hair strewn across my face, my back awash with sweat. It took me a moment to orient myself – mostly because there was no way I could really be where I thought I was.

I brushed the hair off my face – Judi's hair, as it turned out, not mine – and extricated myself from her too-heavy blankets. She slept peacefully beside me, lying on her side, a small smile etched onto her face.

Careful not to wake her, I eased out of bed, oddly self-conscious about being naked, given that no one was awake here to see me. Months ago, I'd left a toothbrush and a stick of deodorant here. I peeked into her bathroom, certain they'd be gone.

They were still there. She'd kept them for me. When she left home yesterday, she hadn't even known I'd come over here – she hadn't put them back there for me. If they were right there where I'd left them, that was because she'd never moved them. As if she'd been waiting for me.

This was too much to handle. My legs going weak, I sat heavily on the toilet, sinking my face into my hands. For four months, I'd thought she hated me. Less than twenty-four hours ago, that was still what I would've said. Now we were back together, and not only had she forgiven me, she'd apologized, too.

I brushed my teeth and took a quick shower, still marveling at the sudden change. If this was too good to be true, how could it possibly last? Judi had probably just been drunk. As soon as she woke up, she'd curse at me and kick me out.

Wrapping myself in one of her soft towels, I ventured back into her room. She blinked her eyes open and looked at me sleepily as I sat next to her on the bed. "I almost thought I dreamed all of it," she said, her voice thick with drowsiness. "I'm so glad you're really here."

"Really? I thought…" I shook my head, leaving the sentence unfinished. Now that the light of day was on us, we needed to have a proper talk about our relationship. "I don't get it, Judi. You hated me so much for so long. How can we snap back to normal as if nothing ever happened?"

"That's not what I'm trying to do. I want to talk about things. We're going to have conversations about what went wrong – a lot of them." Although she looked embarrassed, she put a hand over mine. "In the meantime, all you need to know is that I want to be with you. Desperately."

"Me, too." I turned my hand over, linking my fingers through hers.

"And we have a lot of time to make up for."

I licked my lips, a stir going through my core.

"Yes… yes, we do."

*

Over the next few days, Judi and I had many of the conversations we should've had back when we first broke up. The ones I'd wanted to have, when she'd ignored me instead. To her credit, she apologized time after time for the way she'd shut me out. She said that after a certain point, she'd realized her mistake, but had thought I'd be too angry to want her back. She'd thought I would've moved on.

I held her tight and told her she'd been completely wrong. "There's no one for me but you. Believe me."

Every moment that we weren't at work, we were together, having long conversations and processing our emotions. We told each other a lot of things over those few days, delving deep into our pasts and our subconscious minds to figure out why we'd acted the way we had. At times, it felt like we were psychoanalyzing each other, or ourselves.

Digging that deeply into my psyche, I had realization after realization about my life. I came out of those discussions feeling like I knew myself better than ever before – and I knew her better than I'd ever known another person.

I'd never known a relationship could be like this

– a melding of two minds, two souls meeting and healing each other. I'd always envied the cute couples around me, and I hadn't even known why. Now I could safely say I was as happy, likely happier, than any of them.

My family soon figured out that we were back together. It wasn't much of a mystery, since I'd disappeared for a night – when I'd finally checked my phone that first morning, there were about a million missed calls. They were wary, since they knew how badly Judi had hurt me. But I reminded them I'd hurt her too, and they began to understand.

I spent more and more nights at her place, no longer worried about keeping the relationship from my family. When I came back to pick up clothes about a week after we'd gotten back together, I told my mom straight out, "I'm making up for lost time with her. I might not sleep here too often for a while." Honesty – it was the best policy.

"Just don't forget about us," she said with a wink.

As I headed for the door, Sam came down the stairs to stop me. "Hey," he said. "I just wanted to tell you I'm happy for you and Judi. You two obviously belong together, and it was about time you figured that out."

"I had it figured out this whole time, it was her who needed to catch up. But thanks." I gave him a quick hug. "And thanks for being such a bro about this whole thing. I know it can't have been easy to see me date your crush… or to see me get back with her."

"Honestly, at first it was tougher than I ever let you know." He looked away, then perked up. "Now, though, I've put all of that behind me. I've pretty much forgotten I ever had a thing for Judi. It'll be great to have a cool sister-in-law when you two get married."

"Let's not get ahead of ourselves now."

"And of course I'm a bro," he continued. "I'm your bro." He wrapped me in another hug, a rib-crushing one this time.

I grinned, amazed by my own luck. How was it that I had the world's best partner, *and* such an incredible family? "I hope you'll meet the right girl for you soon, too," I said. "You'd make an awesome boyfriend – to anyone but my woman."

"There's something else I was going to tell you," he said, going suddenly serious. "With my new job, I was thinking I'll get a place of my own. That'll make it easier to date, among other things. I'm twenty-two now. I think it's time."

"You're moving?" I asked, more surprised than I rightfully should've been. Of *course* Sam wouldn't stay in the house with us forever. But as long as I could remember, it'd been me and him – then later Coco, too. "Where are you going to go?"

"You know my buddies Luke and Calvin, who have the share house downtown? A room just opened up, and I think I'm going to take it at the end of this month."

"Wow." This was all happening so fast. Or maybe I would've known earlier if I'd spent more time here this week.

"Don't look so petrified," he laughed. "You'll still see me – I'll come home all the time. And you'll be over at Judi's, anyway. You'll probably be moving in with her soon."

"That's true. Just... everything's changing."

"Things change," he said. "That's part of life. We can only hope that they change in a good way."

"Wise words, little brother. Did you learn them from a video game?"

He rolled his eyes at me. "Funny, big sis. Really funny."

Thirty – Judi

The doorbell rang, and I threw on a bathrobe and ran downstairs to open it. Ella came behind me, twisted up in a sheet, toga-style. Whoever was at the door had certainly picked an inopportune moment to arrive.

A strange man stood on the doorstep, a box in his hands. "Flower delivery for Ms. Judi Nichols."

I signed for it, shaking my head. Once he was gone, I turned back to Ella. "I thought we agreed we weren't going to do anything for *this* one-year anniversary. We were going to wait for one year since we got together for good."

"I couldn't resist," she said, planting a kiss on my cheek. "I thought about where we were this time last year, and I got all mushy inside. Don't worry, I'll get you something better for our real anniversary."

"You could've warned me you were going to do something," I said. "I didn't have a chance to get you something, too."

"It was a last-minute decision. That's why I ordered these online rather than going to a flower shop." She caressed my butt. "You can do something for me some other way."

A throb went through my core, and I bit my lip.

"You mean like taking you out to dinner?" I teased.

"Sure." She rolled her eyes. "Or… something else."

We headed into the kitchen. Luckily Chelle was out, so our lack of clothing wasn't an issue. Chelle had been spending more time at Sabrina's as Ella spent more time here. We all got along, but it was nice to have our own space.

Ella was actually planning to move in here within the next couple of months. Once she did, Chelle would probably find a new place with Sabrina. They'd been together a lot longer than we had, so it only made sense.

"Open it," Ella told me.

I took a knife from the block and carefully sliced through the tape. "Odd to deliver flowers in a box, isn't it?" I murmured to myself as I opened the flaps.

I'd spoken prophetically. The lilies and freesias inside were wilted, some even browning at the edges. "Odd" was the kindest thing that could be said about these flowers. They were on the brink of death!

Turning my face away from Ella so she wouldn't see me cringing, I lifted the vase out of the box. That part was nice, at least. It was a blue-and-white ceramic mosaic, and I could see myself using it for other flowers in the future. Nicer flowers.

"Whoa, those flowers look like shit," Ella said. "I should call the company."

"No, not at all." I fingered a petal. "They're just dry. Once I put some water in here, they'll perk right up."

"You think so?" She frowned at me.

"Yeah. Honey, I love them. Thank you." I wrapped her in a hug, and desire coursed through me at the feeling of her soft skin under my hands. I wanted to rip that sheet right off her.

But she tensed up as she pulled back. "Judi, no one in their right mind would love these flowers. They're half-dead, for heaven's sake."

"A little, but that's okay. This was such a nice gesture."

Her eyebrows shot up, and she stared at me disbelievingly. "You mean you don't love them? You lied to make me feel better?"

I frowned. I hadn't thought about it like that. I'd said I loved them instinctively, without thinking through what I was doing. She was sitting right here looking at them with me. There was no way she would've believed I loved the flowers. "I meant I love that you got them for me," I said.

"That wasn't what you said!" She was clearly thrilled to have caught me in a lie. "You told me you loved the flowers themselves. These dying, wilted, shitty-ass flowers. That was patently untrue."

"I mean…" Heat rose to my cheeks. She'd caught me in a lie. Me, the one who'd made a massive fuss about honesty. The one who'd once thrown out our entire relationship over a lie.

"You said they'd perk up once you put water in them," she said gloatingly. "Do you really believe that, or was that another little white lie?"

I fiddled with the belt of my bathrobe. "Maybe another little white lie," I mumbled.

"So you mean people lie sometimes?" she asked. "Even Ms. Honesty Police herself?"

I huffed, unwilling to answer the question. "How long have you been waiting to catch me in a lie?"

"I wasn't, but now that it's happened, I'm loving it." She nudged me in the ribs. "Just think, ever since we got back together, I've been completely truthful about everything. You, on the other hand – for all I know, you've been lying left, right, and center."

"I haven't!" My blush spread to my neck. I could even see my chest going pink. "This is the first lie, I swear. I just didn't think about what I was saying."

"You know I'm only teasing you, right?" She put her arm around me, and I leaned my head on her shoulder. "The 'no lies ever' policy is a bit over-the-top."

"Okay, I can admit that," I said. "Sometimes they just slip out."

"And I'll be right here to call you on it when they do." She smirked at me. "No more lies, small or big. Ever, until one or the other of us dies."

"That's fine," I said. "You can punish me if you catch me lying." I squeezed her knee, then trailed my fingernails up her bare thigh.

"Hmm… that sounds fair." Her eyes glittered.

I got up and turned on the tap, putting some water in the vase. "By the way, have I mentioned you look terrible when you only wear a sheet?" Coming back, I flicked at the spot where the sheet covered her breasts. "Totally unsexy. It's a real turn-off."

She raised her eyebrows at me. "I think you're lying again."

"And what if I am?" I asked, sliding my hand under the sheet, grazing my palm over her nipple.

"You said I could punish you?" she asked. "I think this deserves a spanking."

She leaned in to press a long, deep kiss against my lips… and then we went upstairs.

Epilogue – Ella

"Welcome, everyone," I said. "The first meeting for the fifth annual Fronton Pride Festival's planning committee will now come to order!"

The people around me quieted down. The room was packed. We'd moved from the library's boardroom to the great hall a couple of years ago, which was annoying because we had to set up rows of chairs before every meeting. Still, the effort was worth it to have this amount of people involved in the festival.

Pride had gotten bigger every year since its inception. Last June, it'd been a two-day event including a parade, a trans pride rally, and a queer women's dance party. I never would've imagined something like this happening in a city of two hundred thousand.

Todd had headed the committee every year until now. He'd moved out of town with his husband, and he'd asked me to run for chair. Although I'd been hesitant, everyone else had encouraged me to run, and I'd finally agreed. And since no one else had run, I'd ended up taking over.

It was all pretty intimidating for a quiet librarian who wasn't used to public speaking. But I'd do my best, and with Judi to support me, I was confident that I'd do okay.

Judi had rushed to get here on time after work. She'd taken a job as a library tech at one of the other Fronton branches, and she was taking part-time online courses toward her master's in library science. She'd be done soon, and my secret hope was that she'd get a job at my location so I could spend all of my days with her.

"A little history for those who might be new," I said, raising my voice louder than I usually spoke. "The first Fronton Pride festival happened five years ago, organized by a group of twelve dedicated volunteers. I was one of them, and volunteering with the festival was the best decision I've ever made. Mostly because that was where I met my wife, Judi." I put my hand on her shoulder.

A chorus of "awws" went through the room.

"If it weren't for Pride, I might've ended up her sister-in-law instead," I said. "But that's a story for another time. My point is that Pride can be rewarding in more ways than one. The festival planning committee is not a singles club... but you never know when you'll meet someone. At the very least, you're bound to make some great new friends."

I noticed some of the younger people shifting in their seats and looking around the room, most likely scanning for potential dates. A few of the older people looked around, too.

"Over the next eight months, we'll be doing a lot

of hard work," I said. "We'll be raising funds, signing up entertainment, getting the word out, and more. If you love Pride and you want to be part of making it happen, you're in the right place. If you have ideas to make Pride even better, or if there's a new event you've always wished we'd put on, this committee is for you."

I glanced at my notes. There was a lot to get through in the next hour. By the end of this meeting, I hoped to have our volunteers broken into subcommittees and for them to have a general idea of what they'd be doing for the rest of the year.

From the front row, Ian gave me an encouraging nod. He had his arm around his new boyfriend. I'd only met the guy few times, but he seemed calm and stable – perfect to balance out Ian's frenetic energy. They had to be pretty serious if they were going to be volunteering together.

The meeting went smoothly, and a few people stopped to talk to me afterwards, telling me how excited they were to help out. Finally, the last of them were gone, and I turned toward Judi. "Ready to go?"

"About time you finished chatting!" she said, audibly exasperated. "We're going to be late for the rehearsal dinner."

"No, we won't." I looked at my watch. Yes, we were.

Judi rolled her eyes. "Don't come crying to me if we miss the entire dinner. Sam's your brother, not mine."

"We'll make it… if we go sixty miles an hour."

We sped our way to the banquet hall where the wedding rehearsal was taking place. Sam and his wife-to-be, Kelly, had been kind enough to delay the rehearsal until after our meeting, and I felt terrible that we were going to make them even later.

Even so, I was overjoyed when I set my eyes on Sam. In his suit and tie, he looked like a real man, not the little boy I still often thought of him as. He was twenty-six now, and he'd been working at his "grown-up job" for around five years.

That was where he'd met Kelly. Even after so long, I still remembered the day he'd told us about her like it was yesterday.

"There's a girl at my job," he said, sitting in the back yard with me, Judi, Mom, and Coco. "We've been flirting a little. I think I'm going to ask her out."

"Not this again," Mom said. "Don't you remember what happened last time?"

"Sure, I remember I found Ella the love of her life." Sam laughed. "This time, the girl's perfect for me."

"What makes you so sure?" I asked.

"She's really sweet and fun, and really pretty too. We make each other laugh. She even likes sports! And she's smart – but not too smart." He shot a glance at Judi.

"She sounds perfect for you," Judi said mildly.

"And you're not going to do anything stupid with this one?" Coco asked snarkily.

"Of course not," Sam said. *"That's why I'm telling all of you – my four favorite women in my life. So that you can help."*

"No!" we all groaned at once.

"Didn't you learn your lesson last time?" I added. *"If you want to win a girl over, you need to be yourself, with no help."*

"It's not going to be like last time," Sam said. *"No one's going to be pretending to be me. I just mean you can give me some advice."*

The four of us shot doubtful looks at one another.

"Some basic, innocent advice," Sam said. *"Like if I should take her to Red Lobster or a steakhouse."*

"I guess we can help," I said. *"But none of us is telling you what to say. No phone calls while you're on your date."*

"I'm way past all of that," he said. *"I only needed that kind of help because Judi was all wrong for me. Kelly's not like that at all. She's the one for me, I swear."*

I hadn't believed him for a second back then – and yet here we were, getting ready for their wedding.

I gave Sam a huge hug, then bestowed one on Kelly. "Sorry we're late. The Pride meeting took a little extra time. There were a bunch of people who wanted to talk to me."

"Not a problem," Kelly said. "We were just waiting for you before we get started. We can't have a rehearsal dinner without one of the bridesmaids, after all." She took Judi by the arm, leading her toward the hall.

I'd worried at first that she'd have an issue with Judi once she knew about Sam's prior "relationship" with her. But Sam had chosen a good woman. Kelly was as sweet and kind as Sam had said from the start, and she'd gotten along with both me and Judi since day one. She had never made an issue of Sam and Judi's one date, and to show that she was truly okay with it, she'd picked Judi as a bridesmaid.

I'd been a tiny bit hurt she hadn't picked me, until she'd pulled me aside and explained her reasoning. Their plan was for me to be Sam's best woman. Coco was a "groomsgirl," and the rest of the wedding party was made up of friends of theirs.

I took Sam's arm as we headed inside. "You found yourself a wonderful woman," I said.

"And kept her around, with your help."

I shook my head. I'd hardly given Sam any advice about Kelly, aside from the obvious things like "ask her about herself" and "bring her chocolate every once in a while." I was no relationship expert. I didn't know how to seduce women or even how to keep them in my life. Finding Judi had been a miracle, a once-in-a-lifetime event, and I gave her the credit for the fact that our relationship was still going strong.

"Anyway, we're even," I said. "I might not have kept Judi if it weren't for you."

"Oh, please. You two were meant to be together." He patted my arm as we reached the door. "Hey, you're not going to talk about the Judi thing during your best woman speech, are you?"

"I'm not making any promises."

We arrived at the head of the table, and I brushed Mom's arm affectionately before sitting down beside her. On the other side of the table, Judi and Kelly were engaged in animated conversation. It warmed my heart to see how close my wife had gotten with my soon-to-be sister-in-law. We were all a happy family now, and I could hardly imagine how things could possibly get any better.

Sam clinked a fork against his glass, bringing everyone's attention to him. The rehearsal was about to begin.

I tried to focus on what he was saying, but all I could think about was that he was right. Judi and I *were* meant to be together.

It was her. It had always been her – from day one, from before I'd even met her.

She was the sun to my moon, the yin to my yang. She made me whole, and she'd made me a better person.

I locked eyes with her from across the table. "I love you," I mouthed.

She put her hand to her heart. "Love you forever," she whispered.

*

I hope you enjoyed reading It Was You!

Sign up to my newsletter at http://eepurl.com/dMjIYo to hear about my new releases.

If you loved the book, please tell your friends! You can also leave a review on Amazon or Goodreads.

Turn the page for a look at my other books.

Thank you for supporting an independent author!

Mother of the Bride

When Gloria's daughter announces she's getting married, Gloria couldn't be happier. Things get more complicated when she realizes the groom's mother was her best friend back in high school - the first woman who ever made her heart beat faster, as well as her first kiss. Gloria and Bethany reconnect during the engagement, and Gloria begins to wonder if she could have her own fairytale romance. Is it too late for Gloria to find love? Or could the mother of the bride be the star of her own story?

Scandalous

Lacey is the last person to be impressed by wealth and fame. Serious and stoic, she values hard work above all else. When she's hired as the home care worker to an injured celebrity, she couldn't care less about Zana's carefully constructed image. She only sees a rich, spoiled brat. Once Lacey and Zana learn to respect each other, they actually get along - and maybe more than that. Can Zana win over the one person who sees the real her?

Two Moms

Being a single mom is far from easy, as both Samantha and Joy know. When Samantha's daughter babysits Joy's son, the women are instantly drawn to each other. Each has her own past, but together they have a chance to create something new. Could these two moms end up starting their own family?

Another Mother

Average suburban mom Sarah is suddenly rocketed into the glitzy world of film when her daughter Emma becomes an actress. The strangest part is seeing gorgeous, glamorous Katie Days pretend to be Emma's mother. Sarah is a normal person and Katie is a celebrity, yet they find common ground in the little girl. Could Emma's fake mom become her other mother?

The Marriage Contract

Twelve years ago, Poppy and Leah vowed to get married if they were both single at thirty. After losing touch, the unlikely pair reconnects just in time to meet the deadline. A lot has happened in twelve years... like both of them coming out of the closet. Now the popular girl marrying the science geek is an actual possibility. The contract was only a joke, though - wasn't it?

Made in the USA
Coppell, TX
16 March 2021